Chill Out!
Breta!

DRUMMOND
ISLAND
DOGMAN

Here's what readers from around the country are saying about Johnathan Rand's AMERICAN CHILLERS:

"Hey! I've read a lot of your boos and I really liked WASH-INGTON WAX MUSEUM. It was the best!"
-Olivia F., age 10, Michigan

"I'm your biggest fan! I read all of your books! Can you write a book and put my name in it?"
-Antonio D.,age 11, Florida

"We drove from Missouri to Michigan just to visit Chillerma-nia!" It's the coolest book store in the world!

-Katelyn H., age 12, Missouri

"Thanks for writing such awesome books! I own every single American Chiller, but I can't decide which one I like best."

-Caleb C., Age 10, New Mexico

"Johnathan Rand is my favorite author in the whole world! Why does he wear those freaky glasses?"

-Sarah G., age 8, Montana

"I read all of your books, but the scariest book was TERRI-FYING TOYS OF TENNESSEE, because I live in Tennes-see and I am kind of scared of toys."
-Ana E., age 10, Tennessee

"I've read all of your books, and they're great! I'm reading CURSE OF THE CONNECTICUT COYOTES and it's AWESOME! Can you write about my town of Vashti, Texas?"

-Corey W., age 11, Texas

"I went to Chillermania on Saturday, April 29th, 2013. I love the store! I got the book THE UNDERGROUND UNDEAD OF UTAH and a MONSTER MOSQUITOES OF MAINE poster and a magic wand. I really want those sunglasses!"

-Justin S., age 9, Michigan

"You are the best author in the universe! I am obsessed with American and Michigan Chillers!"

-Emily N., age 10, Florida

"Last week I got into trouble for reading IDAHO ICE BEAST because I was supposed to be sleeping but I was in bed reading with a flashlight under the covers."

-Todd R., Minnesota

"At school, we had an American Chillers week, and all of the classes decorated the doors to look like an American Chillers book. Our class decorated our door to look like MISSISSIPPI MEGALODON and we won first place! We all got free American Chillers books! It was so cool!"

-Abby T., age 11, Ohio

"When school first started, I read FLORIDA FOG PHANTOMS. Then I got hooked on the series. I love your books!"

-Addison H, age 10, Indiana

"I just finished reading OKLAHOMA OUTBREAK. It was so scary that I thought there was a zombie behind me."

-Brandon C., Florida

"American Chillers books are AWESOME! I read them all the time!"

-Emilio S., age 11, Illinois

"Your books are great! Me and my friend started our own series. Your books should become a TV series. That would be cool!"

-Camerron S., age 9, Delaware

"In first grade, I read Freddie Fernortner, Fearless First Grader. Now I'm reading the American Chillers series, and I love them! My favorite is OREGON OCEANAUTS, because it has a lot of adventure and suspense."

-Megan G., age 12, Arkansas

Got something cool to say about Johnathan Rand's books? Let us know, and we might publish it right here! Send your short blurb to:

Chiller Blurbs
281 Cool Blurbs Ave.
Topinabee, MI 49791

Other books by Johnathan Rand:

Johnathan Rand's
MICHIGAN
CHILLERS

#19: Drummond Island Dogman

Johnathan Rand

An AudioCraft Publishing, Inc. book

This book is a work of fiction. Names, places, characters and incidents are used fictitiously, or are products of the author's very active imagination.

Book storage and warehouses provided by *Chillermania* ©
Indian River, Michigan

Michigan Chillers #19: Drummond Island Dogman
ISBN 13-digit: 978-1-893699-36-6

Librarians/Media Specialists:
PCIP/MARC records available **free of charge** at
www.americanchillers.com

Cover illustration by Dwayne Harris
Cover layout and design by Sue Harring

Printed in USA

DRUMMOND ISLAND DOGMAN

VISIT CHILLERMANIA!

WORLD HEADQUARTERS FOR BOOKS BY JOHNATHAN RAND!

Yooperland

Indian River

Alpena

Traverse City

MICHIGAN

CHILLERMANIA!

**I-75 Exit 313
then south
1 mile!**

Mt. Pleasant

Bay City

Grand Rapids

Lansing

Detroit

Kalamazoo

Visit the HOME for books by Johnathan Rand! Featuring books, hats, shirts, bookmarks and other cool stuff not available anywhere else in the world! Plus, watch the American Chillers website for news of special events and signings at *CHILLERMANIA!* with author Johnathan Rand! Located in northern lower Michigan, on I-75! Take exit 313 . . . then south 1 mile! For more info, call (231) 238-0338. And be afraid! Be veeeery afraaaaaaiiiid . . . .

1

The sky was gray, and the clouds held rain.

"Jackson, are you sure you know where you're going?" Delaney asked loudly. She was seated beside me in the side-by-side off-road vehicle and had to shout over the roaring engine.

"I told you," I said. "I know this land like I know my bedroom. My dad owns over one hundred acres. I grew up here, hiking and riding all over the place. There's no way I can get lost."

"I hope not," Delaney said. "It looks like it's going to rain at any second."

"And that'll make it even *more* fun," I said. "The

trails get all muddy, and we will, too!"

Delaney Granger and I had set out earlier in the afternoon in my side-by-side, which is sort of a souped-up, four-wheel-drive go-kart, designed especially for off-road use. We'd been riding the trails on our property on Drummond Island, Michigan. Drummond Island is, in my opinion, the coolest place anyone could possibly live. I admit that I haven't traveled all over the country, but I've seen and read about some great places. To me, there's no place better than Drummond Island. It's a big island that's part of Michigan's Upper Peninsula. More than two-thirds of the island is owned by the State of Michigan, so it's public property. However, there are only about twelve hundred people who live here. Maybe not even *that* many. The island is named after General Sir Gordon Drummond, Governor-General and Administrator of Canada who died way back in 1854.

There's only one school on the island, and there are only about fifty students. I'm in fifth grade. Delaney is in the same grade, and she's a few months older than me. We met last summer when her family came to the island to help take care of her grandmother. Unfortunately, her grandma passed away over the winter. But Delaney's family loved Drummond Island so much that they decided to move to the island permanently earlier this spring.

There are only three ways you can get to Drummond Island. There is a small airport, but there aren't any commercial airlines. You can arrive by boat, if you have one. Or you can come by car, which is what most people do. So, if you ever want to come to the island with a vehicle, you have to take the ferry from DeTour Village. Cars drive onto the flat, barge-like vessel that safely transports them and their occupants across the St. Mary's River. The distance is about a mile, and the trip across the river takes only about fifteen minutes. My dad and I have been back and forth across the river on the ferry a billion times.

But what I like best about Drummond Island? Animals. There are all sorts of creatures that inhabit the wilds of Drummond Island. Deer, bear, raccoon, squirrels, chipmunks, coyotes, foxes, rabbits, and all sorts of birds. There are even a few moose on the island. The ponds and lakes have frogs, fish, and turtles of all types and sizes.

There is one other kind of animal—a predator—that inhabits the island, although you'll hardly ever see one. I'm talking, of course, about wolves. I've heard there are only a few on the island, but I've never seen them or their tracks. When I was little, I remember hearing them howling one night, and it freaked me out.

So, I don't worry too much about wolves while I'm hiking in the forest or riding the trails in the side-by-side. I don't worry about bears, because they like to keep to themselves, too. In fact, there aren't any animals on Drummond Island that I'm afraid of.

But that was about to change.

2

I carefully needled the side-by-side along a thin trail down a hill, maneuvering around tight corners and over deep, jutting ruts. The knobby, wide tires handled most trails and hills with ease. I was taking Delaney to one of my favorite places: a small pond in a low-lying area, deep within the island.

"Here it is," I said, leaning a bit closer to Delaney so she could hear. As we approached the edge of the pond, I shut off the engine. It spluttered twice and then stopped.

"Pretty cool," Delaney said.

"This is where I found Hops," I said, pointing. "He was right over there."

Two summers ago, I found an injured baby bunny in the weeds near the pond, and I brought him home. He had a bad cut on his leg, and Dad said it looked like he'd been attacked by a fox or a coyote. If that had been the case, it was amazing he'd escaped and was still alive. When I found him, his leg was all torn and bloody. I took him home, cleaned him up, and bandaged his leg. I kept him in a big box for a couple of months while he got better, and then I let him go in the woods. Or, I *tried* to. The problem was that by then, he was too attached to me and wouldn't leave. I even tried taking him way back into the forest, but the next day he'd found his way back. I discovered him in our front yard, hopping around and chewing on grass.

So, he became my pet. I keep him in a big cage in our shed at night, so he won't get eaten by predators. I let him out during the day, and he pretty much just hops around the yard. So, that's what I call him: Hops.

"Are there any fish in the pond?" Delaney asked

as she unbuckled her seat belt, slipped off the seat, and stood. Her long, blonde hair spilled over her shoulders. She was wearing a dark blue sweatshirt with a hoodie, as the October air was a little chilly . . . especially while riding in the off-road vehicle, or ORV. She strode to the edge of the pond.

I, too, climbed out of the side-by-side. My name—Jackson Porter—was stenciled in white paint on the roll bar above the driver's side. Over the summer, the paint had started to chip, and I planned to repaint it soon.

I walked to Delaney's side. "No fish in here," I said, motioning toward the pond with my hand. "Tons of frogs in the summer, though."

I looked up at the gray sky, at the trees shuddering in the cool, fall breeze. It was autumn on Drummond Island, and many of the leaves had started to change color. Green leaves had given way to beautiful shades of yellow, copper, red, orange, and every hue in between. Many had already fallen from their branches, covering the ground like a carpet of colorful gemstones. The leaves that were still on the trees would soon turn brown and die and be torn from the branches by fierce autumn storms.

"Lots of animal tracks here," Delaney said, squatting down on her haunches and pointing to the muddy ground near her feet. "Look at these."

I knelt down to see what she was looking at. There was a trail of very distinct tracks in the soft earth, creating perfect, tiny claw prints.

"Raccoon," I said, very matter-of-factly. Growing up on Drummond Island, I was very familiar with all of the various tracks left by the different animals.

"You can tell just by the tracks?" Delaney asked.

I nodded. "Every animal makes a different track, a different kind of print. See that over there?"

I pointed to yet another set of larger tracks only a few feet away, common tracks I instantly recognized. "That's a deer," I said. "This pond attracts all sorts of animals."

I stood and took a few steps to the left, following the deer tracks as they led to the edge of the pond. Then, they moved along the water's edge. I walked slowly, following them, every so often looking up to scan the bushes that crouched tightly around the pond. The tracks were so fresh that I thought the deer might still be around.

Delaney had moved in the opposite direction, walking the pond's edge.

"Wow," she called out. "I wonder what made these tracks. They're huge. Are they from a bear?"

I turned and walked to her, stopping at her side.

I looked at the tracks in the soft earth.

I blinked and looked again.

I rubbed my eyes. Stared.

Delaney sensed my uneasiness.

"What?" she asked. "What's wrong? Are they bear tracks?"

I ignored her. Not intentionally, of course, but I was too fascinated—too stunned—by what I was seeing to respond to her question.

These aren't bear tracks, I thought. My heart was racing as I inspected the tracks. *They must be wolf tracks.*

My heart hammered.

Wolf tracks?

Impossible. These tracks are bigger than my feet. Wolf tracks would be half this size. These tracks weren't made by a—

A tingle of horror slithered beneath my skin, wrapping around my muscles and flowing through my bloodstream. A terrifying, nightmarish vision came to mind.

No. No, it couldn't be. That's just a myth. A made-up story.

Unless—

Just thinking the word in my mind sent a wave of horror streaking through my arteries, filling my heart with dread. My head pounded.

One word.

Just two syllables.

A two syllable word that made me dizzy with fear, icing my skin with terror-chill.

The word?

Dogman.

3

It had been some time since the creature had eaten, and he was hungry. He stood on all fours nestled in the pines near the pond. His body was relaxed but alert. Beneath his rough, wiry fur, tight muscles were unstrained but ready. Ready to spring, to run, to pursue.

Ready to hunt.

He sniffed the air with his sensitive nose. He was able to detect dozens of various scents, but nothing pleasing to his palate, nothing that would satisfy his hunger. He'd followed the scent of a deer to the pond, but the animal had been spooked and fled. A deer would have been tasty, a nice filling meal. But deer were fast and required speed and effort to chase down. So—

He waited.

He listened.

Through the wind in the trees, another sound came. Although it was faint, it was unpleasant and irritating to the beast. It was a droning sound, steady, then rising in pitch, then falling.

And it was getting closer.

Still, he was patient, sniffing the air for any new smells.

Nothing.

Yet.

The sound drew nearer. Louder.

The creature bared his teeth, but uttered no sound. His muscles tightened; his eyes scanned the forest.

Still, the sound grew louder. The creature did not like the sound. It was noise, unwelcome and invasive. It made him angry. The noise was unnatural, mechanical, intrusive.

But the noise also meant—

Meat.

Food.

The beast turned, slinking along the side of the pond at an unrushed but steady gait.

And the noise drew nearer.

The creature, enormous in size even on all fours, slipped silently through the thick brush and crouched low. Peering through the branches, he caught a glimpse of movement. The sound of the machine ceased, only to be replaced by another sound.

Voices.

Humans.

Tucked in the shadows, hunkered to the ground, the beast watched.

And waited.

4

"Are they bear tracks?" Delaney asked again. I hadn't responded to her question.

Instead, I glanced up and looked around the pond, searching the gauzy, black shadows, the hidden alcoves and dark caverns nestled within the spiny branches and colorful autumn leaves.

My mind and body were on full alert, and I wasn't sure why. I wasn't sure why I'd broken into a chilled sweat, and I wasn't sure why I was suddenly so nervous. I wasn't sure what was lurking in the shadows, if anything, and I wasn't sure what type of animal had made those huge, claw-like tracks in the mud near the pond.

But I had an idea. Sure, maybe it was just my imagination getting the best of me.

Still—

"We have to leave," I said coldly. "We have to leave, and we have to leave *now.*"

"What?" Delaney asked, her eyes darting around nervously. "What's wrong?"

I didn't want to say anything. I didn't want to tell her that the tracks we'd found didn't belong to a bear.

A wolf?

No. If the tracks belonged to a wolf, it would have to be the biggest wolf in the world.

And there it was again, the thought tucked away in the back of my mind, a thought I didn't want to entertain, something I didn't want to think about. And yet, the thought kept coming back to me, knifing through my mind, emerging from the darkness and casting a shadow over my soul.

Dogman.

Don't be silly, I told myself. *Dogman isn't real.*

He's just a legend. A story. Everybody knows that.
Don't they?

Don't they?

Like it or not, I would soon get my answer. And
it wasn't the answer I was hoping for.

5

The beast was hungry, and the scent of human flesh drove him crazy. He sniffed the air slowly, his nostrils flaring, and he was careful not to make a single sound. His mouth was open, exposing rows of enormous, sharp teeth, wet with saliva. A loop of drool fell from his lower jowl and landed silently on a leaf.

And the creature could hear them now, communicating in that garbled language that he could not understand, language that he'd heard often. But in the same way a human cannot understand what a dog says when he barks or growls, the beast could not possibly know what these two small humans were saying to one another. The only thing the creature knew was that they were young. He knew they would not be able to run as fast as he. He knew that it had been a full day since he'd had anything to eat, and he knew these humans smelled *delicious.*

Still, he also knew he had to be cautious. After all: he hadn't survived as long as he had by making mistakes that would get him caught, mistakes that would bring other humans into the woods to search for him, to hunt him down like—

—*an animal.*

A *beast.*

A freak of nature that shouldn't exist, but *did.*

He watched from the shadows as the female species knelt next to the pond, a mane of golden hair flowing over her shoulders. She spoke in a raised voice, and this brought the male species to her side. The creature waited, motionless, as the two humans inspected something at their feet.

A breeze came, again bringing the delicious human scent to the beast's sensitive nose. He savored the moment as if drinking in a delicacy, a taste to be cherished.

Two young, small humans, alone, in the forest. There were no other humans around and none of their square-shaped dens in which they could safely retreat.

There was only them . . . and him.

Alone.

He lifted a huge paw, a long claw that had the qualities of both a human and a dog.

Slowly.

Silently.

He paused.

He waited.

He sniffed the air.

And somewhere deep within the creature, a desperate hunger growled and snarled.

It was time to attack.

6

The feeling of dread was so overwhelming that I grabbed Delaney's hand and dragged her to the side-by-side.

"What?" Delaney asked as she stumbled to keep her balance. She tried to jerk her hand away, but I wouldn't let go. "Jackson! Will you tell me what's wrong?"

"I'll tell you when we get on our way," I replied. I snapped my head around, peering into the shadows.

A branch moved.

"Get in the machine!" I ordered Delaney.

"All right, all right," she huffed, slipping into the passenger seat and fastening her seat belt. I punched the start button, and the engine roared to life.

"Hang on!" I shouted, slipping my own seat belt over my shoulder and buckling it to the metal clasp next to my hip. I stepped on the accelerator pedal and hungry tires dug into the earth, throwing mud and gravel and pieces of branches into the air behind us. In seconds, we were racing along the trail as fast as I could safely go. Still, I kept looking behind me, glancing over my shoulder, not knowing what I would see behind us, hoping that there would be nothing there. Hoping I was wrong.

By now, Delaney was getting agitated. Not because of anything I'd done or said, but because of what I *hadn't* said. I hadn't responded to her persistent question about bear tracks. Instead, I had ignored her and simply ordered her to the side-by-side without saying anything. I know I wasn't being very polite, but at the moment, I didn't want to waste any time trying to explain what I was thinking or feeling. In fact, I didn't know *myself* what I was thinking or feeling. Maybe it was silly, maybe it wasn't. But I had a hunch, a sixth sense, that kept whispering in my ear, telling me to get away as fast as we could.

And I don't really know how to explain it. I hadn't spotted anything in those shadows. I hadn't heard anything. Yet, my inner danger alarm, a warning bell inside my head, had been set off by something.

What?

For whatever reason, I had the feeling that we were being watched. No, worse than that. Not only did I know that we were being watched, but I knew that whatever was watching us was getting ready for something. I had never had such a strong feeling like that, ever.

So, with Delaney riding beside me, I piloted the side-by-side along the trail. The farther we traveled, the better I felt. I'm not sure what we had escaped or what we'd left behind, but I somehow knew that we had narrowly escaped with our lives.

7

The beast burned with anger. He'd made a mistake and hesitated for too long. He'd missed his chance. He had sprung from his hiding place just as the terrible-sounding machine tore away, spewing damp earth into the air. For a moment, he'd thought about giving chase, but he knew that, often, machines could travel faster than he could. He could chase after his prey, but there was a good chance that he would not be able to keep up. He would lose them. There would be danger in that, he knew. Humans were different from other animals. Humans processed thoughts, had the ability to reason, not unlike his own ability.

However, his ability to reason was limited, although enhanced by his animal-like qualities: a super-sensitive nose and ears, keen eyesight, and incredible strength. In most cases, he had a tremendous advantage over his prey.

Except for humans.

Humans, with their ability to think and plan, could cause problems for him. They had in the past. It was one of the reasons he'd come to this island in the first place. He'd been hunted by humans for far too long, and he knew that it would be only a matter of time before they outsmarted him with their search parties and machines and weapons.

No, he'd needed a place where he could hide, a forested area he could inhabit without the constant threat of humans, a place where he could be the hunter and not the hunted.

So, he'd come to Drummond Island. His sharp senses knew the direction to travel, knew where to go in the same way birds knew which direction to fly in the spring and summer. Instinct drew him north, out of Wexford County in Michigan's Lower Peninsula and up through the forests of Grayling and the AuSable River region. He spent some time in Wolverine, nearly a year, before being drawn farther north to Mackinaw City, where he'd faced another problem: how to cross the Straits of Mackinac, a berth of water several miles wide, where Lake Michigan and Lake Huron met. The Mackinac Bridge? It was open only to traffic, and with its many lights, he would be spotted immediately. He was capable of swimming, but he knew that the long, arduous swim across the Straits would require time and effort, leaving him exhausted. No, it would be much better to find an easier way, a route that wouldn't expend so much valuable energy.

So, he'd found a place to hide in the space of an empty semi trailer. He'd waited in the shadows beyond a parking lot, emerging cautiously to try trailer after trailer until he'd found one with an unlocked door. Once inside, he hid among the various stacks of boxes and crates. This provided him a way to cross the mighty Mackinac Bridge.

Hours later the driver of the large vehicle had stopped at a roadside park along US-2 to rest for a moment; the police never found his body. All they found were deep, angry scratch marks on the door of the semi truck and a few bits of long, scraggly hair stuck to the vehicle's mirror. Dogman had fled, slipping into the deep, dark woods. Instinct drew him east, until he'd reached the sleepy community of DeTour Village and the one-mile span of the St. Mary's River. An easy swim in the cover of night.

And on the other side of the river—

Sanctuary.

A new home.

A place where he could hide and be safe. A place where he could live on his terms, where he could thrive.

A place where he could hunt.

8

Finally, after we'd traveled a safe distance, far enough from the pond that I was certain we hadn't been followed—

By what?

I slowed the side-by-side to a stop at the edge of the forest. Ahead of us was a flat, wide stretch of alvar. Alvar is made up of limestone, often covered by a thin layer of soil where grass and small plants grow. It was formed millions of years ago by wind whipping all the topsoil away, leaving only the bare limestone. In some places, it looks like old, cracked cement. On Drummond Island, there's a huge area called the Maxton Plains, which is made up of alvar. The area is flat, for the most part, and there are trails and two-tracks that thread throughout the region. Lots of tourists come to the Maxton Plains for sightseeing, hiking or biking, or running the trails with off-road vehicles.

"What was that all about back there?" Delaney asked. "Why were you so freaked out?"

I didn't want to lie to Delaney, but I didn't want her to be frightened, either. And I certainly wasn't going to say the word 'Dogman.' Oh, I was pretty sure she'd heard about the legend and the stories, but I had no proof of anything. I didn't even know myself. The only thing I knew was that we'd found some huge tracks near the pond, tracks that I wasn't familiar with, tracks that were too big to be made by a bear or a wolf. A moose? No way. Moose tracks are big, but they look totally different from what we saw at the pond.

So, I told Delaney the truth. I just didn't tell her everything.

"I don't know," I replied. "I just had a weird feeling that we were being watched."

"I did, too," Delaney admitted. "Those tracks kind of freaked me out."

"They were fresh, too," I said. "Whatever made them had been in the area right before us."

"Maybe it was still around, watching us," Delaney said.

"Maybe," I said.

And suddenly, I didn't want to talk about it anymore. I was getting freaked out all over again, and I didn't like that crawling, uneasy feeling, the feeling I'd had back at the pond.

So, I changed the subject. Delaney had never been on this part of the island before, and while we sat on the idling side-by-side, I told her what I knew about Maxton Plains and how the region was formed.

"Back on our property, there's a place Dad and I call 'Lookout Ledge.' It's a ridge at the top of a hill. From it, you can look out and see over Sturgeon Bay and the St. Mary's River. All sorts of islands, too."

"I thought Drummond Island was in Lake Huron," Delaney said.

"It is, sort of," I replied. "The waters are the same. The smaller bodies of water have different names. But you're right: all of the waters belong to

43

Lake Huron. And you can see for miles and miles from Lookout Ledge."

"That sounds awesome!" Delaney said.

"It is," I said. "And the trails to get to it are a blast to ride."

"I can't wait," Delaney said.

We continued chatting and soon forgot all about Dogman.

But not for long.

9

The sun was sinking in the west, so we made our way through the forest and back to town. I dropped off Delaney at her house and told her I'd see her in the morning. Both of us didn't live too far from school, so we walked there every day.

I parked the side-by-side in our garage on the right side. We have a two-car garage; Dad parks his truck on the left side, and we store the side-by-side on the right. However, it was still early, and Dad wasn't home. He had said that he had to go to St. Ignace for the day and would be catching the five-forty ferry from DeTour Village. That meant he would probably be home around six-fifteen.

I went to the shed to check on Hops. The bottom hinge of the shed door had finally rusted away, and now I had to lift up on the handle to get it open. I carefully lifted and pulled, opened it all the way, and then leaned it against the outer wall. Dad said he'd grab a new hinge at the hardware store in St. Ignace.

"Hey, Hops old pal," I said to the rabbit in the cage. His cage door, like the shed, was broken. In fact, if he wanted to, Hops could easily get out simply by pushing on the little metal door. However, he'd never figured it out, so I wasn't worried about it. Besides: from the outside of the cage, it wasn't possible to open unless you lifted the steel latch. I wasn't worried about a fox or coyote figuring that out, which was why I kept Hops in the cage, anyway.

Hops scampered out, and I left him to bounce around on his own, free to exit the shed and nibble on bits of grass and bounce around the yard. I took the two dishes from his cage, filled one with rabbit food, and took the other inside to give him a fresh bowl of water. When I returned, Hops was sitting in the grass just outside the open door of the shed, gnawing on blades of grass.

"How's the salad?" I asked as I walked past him and went into the shed. I put his water bowl in his cage, and then I heard gravel crunching.

Dad's home, I thought, and I left the shed in time to see Dad's truck pulling into the driveway. I waved, and as he passed, he grinned and held up a pizza box for me to see.

Awesome. Another gourmet dinner, courtesy of Dad's Take-Out Diner.

"No pizza for you, buddy," I said to the rabbit, and I reached down and gave Hops a scratch behind his ears. Then, I left him to his organic treat and went inside to have pizza with Dad and to tell him about the tracks we'd spotted at the pond.

Unfortunately, I completely forgot that I hadn't put Hops back in his cage. That was something I'd remember in the middle of the night . . . when it was almost too late.

10

In the kitchen, I told Dad about the tracks we'd spotted. The two of us sat at the dining room table, gobbling pizza.

"It might have been a wolf, you know," he said.

I shook my head, took a moment to chew a mouthful of pizza, and then spoke.

"No," I replied. "The tracks were too big. They were bigger than my foot."

"Well, that could have been caused by the soft ground," Dad said. "If the animal was moving, the tracks might appear larger than they are. My guess is that you probably surprised him. Wolves really don't want much to do with people, especially people riding off-road vehicles. He probably took off running when he heard you coming, making his tracks appear bigger as he ran."

What Dad was saying seemed to make sense. Maybe the tracks *did* belong to a wolf. Maybe we had surprised the animal, like Dad suggested. Which was too bad. I would have liked to have seen a wolf in the wild.

Still, there was that nagging feeling inside me that said a single word, a disagreeable word, a word I didn't like. Not at that particular moment, anyway.

No.

No.

The word went around my head while Dad was explaining that the tracks we'd spotted, most likely, belonged to a wolf.

No.

No.

I knew better.

Did I?

I wasn't sure I agreed with Dad, but I wasn't

sure that I was right, either. Dad's explanation seemed to be the most reasonable, the most logical. My idea—Dogman—seemed farfetched, something out of fantasy land or a movie. Or a book. There's a guy somewhere in Michigan who writes creepy stories about things in different parts of the state. Aliens, ghosts, dinosaurs . . . things like that. Crazy things. Things that couldn't possibly be true, not by a long shot. Oh, he says they're all true stories, but they're not.

That's what my idea sounded like.

Fiction.

Fantasy.

Something dreamed up from someone's crazy imagination. Something that couldn't possibly be true.

But that night, something would happen that gave me a pretty good indication that maybe what I was experiencing on Drummond Island *wasn't* fiction, at all. It wasn't made up, it wasn't legend or folklore. It wasn't fantasy, it wasn't make-believe.

It was *real.*

11

One in the morning.

My room was dark. I don't have a night light in my bedroom, and I sleep with the door closed because Dad is usually up late, watching television. The noise keeps me up, because I'm a pretty light sleeper. Any sound at all can wake me, and it can be pretty annoying sometimes, because then I often find it hard to get back to sleep.

But Dad goes to bed around eleven-thirty. He turns off all the lights except for a tiny night light on the wall in the bathroom. The house becomes silent and catlike, nestled safely within itself. I've never been afraid of the dark, especially in our house. The darkness, it seemed to me, was comforting. It felt like protection, a sentry against anything that might be—

What?

Outside?

No, that's not it. I wasn't afraid of anything outside or in the woods, even after dark.

Maybe I just felt safer in our house after dark. The quiet, the calm, the peace of night seemed to ease any lingering troubles of the day. It was as though the darkness was telling me to rest, that tomorrow was a new day, a better day.

But now, something had caused me to stir—some odd noise of some sort—beyond my bedroom window.

And there it was again. A ruffling, shuffling sound.

Gone. Silence.

Stillness.

Again. Louder this time. More insistent.

I sat up in bed, leaned over to the window, and peeled back the curtain a crack. Of course, it was impossible to see anything in the darkness. We don't have any outside lights, and on this particular night, the moon was obscured by a thick layer of clouds.

I slowly slid the window open, and crisp, clean air licked at my face. October nights get cold on Drummond Island, a warning that winter is on its way.

There it was again. A fluttering commotion, like paper slapping paper in three quick successions.

Swishswishswish.

I didn't recognize the sound, but there were any number of animals it could be. I was glad that Hops was safely—

Hops!

I suddenly remembered that I hadn't put him back in his cage, that I'd left him out with the shed door wide open!

12

I flung the sheets away, nearly throwing them off the bed. My feet hit the carpet, and in an instant, I was at my closet where I fumbled for the light. I found my slippers and hastily pulled a sweatshirt over my head. I might look silly wearing pajama pants and a sweatshirt with a college emblem on the front, but I doubted anyone was going to see me in front of our house at one o'clock in the morning!

I hurried out of my bedroom and through the murky darkness of the hallway. The only light came from the faint glow of the night light in the bathroom, but it was enough for me to find my way without smacking into a wall.

In the kitchen, we have what Dad calls a 'junk drawer.' It's just a lot of odds and ends that don't have any particular place. The drawer is cluttered with keys, slips of paper, a few receipts, small tools, a half pack of gum, a bottle of aspirin, pens and pencils, a half-squished tube of glue, and about a dozen other, various things.

And a flashlight.

I pawed through the jumble until I found the cylinder-shaped object about the size of my fist. Light burst forth, and I followed the beam's splatter on the carpet as I hustled to the garage door, through the garage, and into the front yard.

Again, cold air washed over me. It wouldn't be long before our entire yard was covered with several feet of fluffy, white snow.

But not tonight. Tonight the cool grass was wet and squishy, and I swept the beam back and forth, left to right, up and down, searching.

And there was the noise again.

Swishswishswish.

It was coming from behind the shed.

I remembered the tracks Delaney and I had found at the pond earlier that day. I remembered the scary feeling of being watched by some unseen predator and the very real sense of danger that made me pull Delaney to the side-by-side and flee.

It might have been a wolf, you know, Dad had said.

That would be bad enough. But deep down, I knew Dad was wrong. The tracks we'd found didn't belong to a wolf, I was sure.

So, what kind of animal made them? What kind of animal was making that strange noise behind the shed? Most important: where was Hops? Was I too late to save him?

I rushed forward, my slippers sliding on the dew-covered grass. The wide beam of light settled on the short growth of pine trees at the side of the shed. Shadows crawled.

"Hops?" I called out.

Swishswishswishswish . . . .

I reached the shed door and shined the light behind the structure. There was a movement near the back wall of the shed.

Before I could move my light, before I could train the beam on it, the beast attacked. The only thing I glimpsed were two horrifying, glowing eyes as they came directly at me. The flashlight was knocked from my hand and went out. I stumbled back, tripped, and fell, helpless and defenseless, to the cold ground.

13

I hit the ground flat on my back as I drew my arms up to protect my face. The fall knocked the wind out of me, and I struggled to gulp in cool air as the monster—

Monster?

No.

The beast that attacked me hadn't been a beast, after all. It was a very large bird, an enormous, great horned owl. They hunt at night, and although they're not often seen, they're not an uncommon bird on Drummond Island or anywhere else in Michigan, for that matter. They eat just about any animal they can overtake, including rats, mice, voles, even reptiles. But their favorite food is—

I quickly rolled to my side and pawed the grass until I found the flashlight. I clicked it on and leapt to my feet.

Rabbits, I thought, the horror hitting me like a football linebacker. *The favorite food of the great horned owl is rabbit.*

"Hops?" I called out, frantically sweeping the beam along the grass and the side of the shed. "Where are you?"

I was overwhelmed by relief when I heard a shuffling sound and saw a twitching nose pop out from the small space beneath the shed and the ground. Hops emerged with several quick bounces, stopping at my slippers.

I bent down. "Oh, man," I said, gently scooping up the rabbit by the scruff of his neck. I held him in my arms, tightly to my chest. "I thought you were a goner. Sorry I left you to fend for yourself."

I returned the rabbit to his cage and closed the shed door, still in disbelief. I had been lucky. Great horned owls are perhaps one of the best—if not *the* best—night time predators around. Rabbits are easy kills for great horned owls, and it was only by chance that Hops had somehow escaped capture. I doubt the bunny knew how close he'd come to being owl food.

But the great horned owl wasn't the only predator prowling nearby, lurking in the shadows. I didn't realize I wasn't alone . . . until I heard a twig snap.

14

The smells of night filled his nostrils, and although most would say the night was quiet, the inhuman beast's acute sense of hearing picked up many things. The breath of a mouse. The crawling of a shrew. The sound of a television over a half-mile distant. Sounds that could never be heard by human ears.

A ruffle of wings.

A frantic scattering of leaves.

More fluttering . . . .

Another predator was at work, on patrol in the

silent, mystical hours.

Dogman waited in silence.

More fluttering, not far away. He heard the terrified, high-pitched squeal of an animal, a rabbit, perhaps, and then more fluttering. Nearby, a frantic scattering of leaves and small twigs. The creature was close to the commotion. A large bird had been hunting from the sky, swooping down, closing in for a kill.

And then—

Another sound.

A click and a swish.

A small light.

Soft, hurried footsteps on grass.

The beast's ears stood straight and stiff, his senses on high alert.

A scent came to his nose, familiar, delicious, tantalizing.

The smell of a human.

The light came closer, sweeping all around. Once, it was aimed directly at the beast, but he knew that he was hidden a safe distance away, crouched in the shadows of the thick branches, leaves, and pine needles. He could not be seen.

But *he* could see. *He* could watch.

He saw the small human cry out during a mash of chaotic sound and confusion, heard him fall to the ground. The light faltered. The beast's heart hammered, and he nearly sprang from the shadows, knowing that he could easily overtake the human in his moment of weakness.

But he waited. The creature was, above all, cunning. Smart. Intelligent. He knew when to strike.

The small human stood, and the light clicked on.

The night was silent.

The beast, crouched in his hiding place, haunches tight, muscles ready, brain engaged, shifted his weight the tiniest bit. A small, dry twig no bigger than a toothpick, snapped beneath his foot.

15

I heard the snap of a twig just after I'd closed and latched the shed door. It caused me to stop, to freeze in my tracks, motionless. The flashlight beam was trained on the trees a few feet away.

I waited.

Listened.

Nothing.

Not a single sound.

That, in itself, seemed strange. In the summer, the night is filled with various noises, such as the chirping of crickets and the rhythmic croaking and peeping of frogs. Dad and I live outside of the village, so there aren't any cars going by. And rarely do we hear a plane, especially at night.

But now it was October. All of the insects were gone, the frogs and toads in hibernation for the long winter that would soon be upon us.

Yet, the complete and absolute silence I was experiencing was discomforting. It was as though all of the night creatures had been frightened into hiding, as if they had scurried back to their homes and dens to escape some unseen force or unknown predator.

I continued listening. I was certain I'd heard something nearby, a snapping of a branch or the crunching of a dry, brittle leaf.

My imagination went into overdrive, like it had done at the pond when Delaney and I had discovered the large tracks in the soft earth. I had been filled with a feeling of overwhelming dread, a feeling of increasing dire. My instincts had warned me that something was very, very wrong, that it was time to flee, to get away from the area as quickly as possible.

That same feeling came over me as I stood frozen in the darkness. Although the night air was cool, my skin felt hot and clammy. A thin sheen of sweat had formed, despite the chilly temperature.

The silence roared.

Not another sound was heard.

I slowly shifted the flashlight beam to the left and then to the right. Up, down. Around.

Nothing.

Not a single sound.

I remembered the glowing eyes of the owl as the bird had flown directly at my face. I'd surprised him, and no doubt he was just as afraid of me as I was of him.

But now, this was something else. There was something in the darkness, something unseen, that had eyes just as penetrating as the owl's. I was certain of it. I could feel the eyes in the night; I could sense them in the darkness, watching me. The same eyes that had been watching Delaney and me from the shadows near the pond. Watching, waiting. Waiting for just the right moment . . . .

I wasn't going to give it a chance, whatever it was. I took off running, taking giant steps across the lawn, the flashlight beam bouncing wildly. Shadows leaped and flew in every direction. Into the garage, past Dad's sleeping truck. I'd left the garage door cracked open, and I slowed just enough so that I wouldn't crash into it and wake Dad. I quietly closed and locked the door behind me.

Safety.

The relief of being in my own home, safe and secure, felt as though a heavy weight had been lifted from my shoulders. The panic I'd felt moments before began to dissipate and fade. My breathing returned to normal.

Home. Inside.

I tiptoed across the carpet, and the only sound was the soft shushing of my slippers. After getting a glass of water from the kitchen, I returned to my room, stepped out of my slippers, pulled off my sweatshirt, and climbed into bed. I closed the window, but not before giving one more glance outside, into the darkness, into the shadows and mystery and fright I'd just left behind.

Nothing but an ink-black wall and its cryptic secrets.

I fell asleep in the safety and comfort of my bed, glad to be indoors, glad I'd been able to get to Hops just in time before the great horned owl had made a meal out of him. Glad that whatever was in the woods beyond the shed—if it was anything at all—was out there. Outside. And I was inside.

Just my imagination, I thought as I drifted off to sleep. *That's all it was. My imagination.*

Unfortunately, the beast stalking the woods of Drummond Island had nothing to do with my imagination. Dogman—the horrifying creature that was supposed to be only a legend—was about to walk straight out of my nightmares . . . and into reality.

16

He had waited; he had watched. He had considered making his move, bursting from the shadows, snaring the small human in his enormous claws.

No.

His instinct spoke to him, and he listened. He was hungry, but caution spoke louder than his need for food.

Had the small human spotted him? No. He watched the boy as he stood motionless, holding the light device, moving it around. The beast could sense the small human's fear, carried in the gentle night wind. He could taste it.

At that moment, he could have easily overtaken the boy. It would have taken mere seconds.

Still—

No. The time wasn't right. He would wait for a better time, a better opportunity.

But when the boy began running, leaping across the lawn in giant leaps and bounds, the beam of light careening wildly, the creature found himself following. His hulking figure emerged from the forest just as the boy vanished into the shadows of the garage. He heard a door slam. Continuing on along the front of the house, he sniffed the air, following the human scent as it drifted through an open window.

Dogman was only a few feet from the screen. He could hear shuffling inside. His night vision was much better than a human's. He saw the boy's face through the screen and knew that he, himself, although only a few feet from the house, could not be spotted.

The window slid closed behind the screen, and the curtain covered it. Dogman waited for a moment and then sniffed the air again.

There it was again. The smell of a small animal. He turned slowly, sniffed the air.

Quietly, he stalked toward the shed.

17

The shed door was open.

I stopped in the driveway, carrying my backpack over one shoulder. Dad had already headed off to work, and I was on my way to school.

And the shed door was wide open.

Didn't I close it last night? I wondered. *Yes, I did. I'm sure of it. It was closed when I got scared and ran back into the house. But Dad probably needed something before he left for work.*

I turned and strode to the shed. With every step

I took, a knot of trepidation twisted my stomach. Something was wrong, I was sure of it. I could *feel* it.

The shed door had scratches on the outside. Several deep gashes—claw marks—were dug into the wood near the handle. It was as though something had struggled to get the door open, pawing at the handle until it succeeded.

Inside the shed, nothing looked amiss. Hops was in his cage, looking at me, his jaws moving back and forth, his whiskers twitching.

"Good morning, fuzzy buddy," I said to the rabbit. I checked to make sure he had enough food and water, and then I returned to the door to inspect the gashes again.

Common sense told me it was the work of a bear. My imagination—something I should never listen to, but often did—told me something else.

I looked at the ground, searching for tracks. Here, by the shed, the grass grew tight and trim, so there weren't any clear imprints of anything. In several spots, the grass appeared to be pressed down, but I could have done that with my shoes.

"Be good," I told my rabbit in the cage. "I'll see you after school."

I closed the shed door.

The morning was cool and crisp, and I pulled my coat collar around my neck to keep warm on my walk. We have a long, two-track driveway that leads out to Townline Road. And although I had a math test that day, it was the farthest thing from my mind as I hiked up the winding driveway. No, I was thinking of other things.

Strange things.

Weird things.

I was thinking about bizarre tracks, bigger than my feet, that we'd discovered at the pond the day before. I was thinking about the strange feeling that Delaney and I were being watched from the shadows of the forest. I thought about how silent it had been overnight, when I went to check on Hops. How the stillness seemed to be alive with a dark, foreboding, unseen presence.

I was thinking, in short, about Dogman.

I know he's not real, I told myself. *The whole thing is just made up. All the stories, all the fables and legends . . . it's all just make-believe.*

Or was it?

I think nobody really knew for sure. After all:

stories, no matter how crazy or farfetched, usually begin with a seed of truth, a nugget of something that is real. However, as the story gets passed along and retold, it tends to change, buoyed by the imagination of each person who's doing the telling.

Regardless of whether or not the stories of Dogman were true, I found myself walking at a faster pace than normal as I made my way up our long driveway. I would be alone until I reached the open expanse of Townline Road, where I would, most likely, see a few friends on the way to school. And I would, of course, meet up with Delaney, and we would walk the rest of the way to school together.

But now . . . .

The trees around me were filled with candy-colored leaves of copper, amber, crimson, and gold, all sugar-coated with glittering, frozen morning dew. The branches and limbs knitted together to create a tunnel of shadow magic, and as I walked, frosty leaves crunched beneath my feet. The sound reminded me of bones being gnawed by powerful jaws and long, sharp teeth.

Crunch went the leaves under my shoes.

Crunch.

Crunch.

Was I being watched?

Crunch.

Was there someone—something—watching me at that very moment, hiding behind the colorful leaves and woven branches?

Crunch.

I walked faster.

Crunch.

Crunch.

Finally, I made it to Townline Road. A few minutes later, Delaney and I were walking together to school.

I felt safe—for the time being.

18

The beast watched from the shadows. His hunger had been quenched hours earlier in the pre-dawn gloom, when he'd discovered a dumpster behind a restaurant that had been filled with food scraps from the previous day. The garbage bin was filled with bits of hamburgers, steak, french fries, hot dogs, pizza, and bread. An easy, delicious meal, although he'd had to remain watchful, careful to remain out of sight, careful that he wasn't spotted, afraid of making any noise. He didn't want to bring attention to himself, as that would only mean trouble. Stealth and surprise were his allies. In the darkness before the dawn, he'd been able to gorge on the morsels until he was filled.

But soon, he knew, his hunger would return. It always did, and it always would. Such was the way of life for man and beast . . . and he was both.

Now, as the sun rose from the east and chased away the ghost shadows of night, the huge beast crouched low to the ground on all fours, watching, motionless, from the forest. Children passed by on the road, along with those infernal, smelly, metal machines that made such maddening noise. Around him, the birds of the forest awakened and talked with one another. Although he could not understand what they were saying, he knew the birds did not fear him, nor was he ever a threat to them. They went about their morning rituals as they did every day, along with every other creature in the forest, and even the humans in their box-like dens. There were patterns to life, and in these patterns, familiarity.

And the beast grew to know these patterns and became familiar with them himself. He knew more about most humans than they knew about themselves, and that made him all the more cunning and wary. It kept him cautious and alert, and for those reasons, he had lived long without much interference. Of course, there were recent times when human intrusion became more than an annoyance, which was the reason he'd escaped to the safety of Drummond Island, a place where he could live and hide among the regions of vast forests and dense thickets.

A place where he could hunt.

And feed.

He watched as another child, alone, walked along the shoulder of the road. Safely tucked in the shadows and branches, the beast was only a few feet from the defenseless girl. He could be upon her in seconds.

No. The time was not right.

He lowered to the ground, curling his lips and snarling softly.

And waited.

19

I nearly failed.

I did the best I could, I guess, but I have to admit that I hadn't studied, and I'd never been very good in math. Or maybe that wasn't it. Maybe I *could* be good in math, but I never applied myself to the task. I never really tried. That was, most likely, the reason I have never been good with numbers.

But whatever the reason, I nearly failed the test. I received a D minus, the lowest grade I'd ever received on any test in my life.

However, my teacher was pretty cool about it. She said that she was disappointed, that she thought I was a good student, but I really needed to get focused on my schoolwork. She said I could do one of two things: I could let the test grade stand as it was (not good) or try taking the test again at the end of the week. She said that if I studied, I could do much better, and my grade would reflect it. And she said she would throw out the D minus as though it never happened.

Although I wasn't looking forward to cramming for the test, it sounded much better than having a D minus on my test record. My end-of-the-year school grade depended on many of these little exams, and a couple of bad results could really make a difference.

So, if I could take the test over, do better and bring my grade up, that would be a huge help.

"I'll help you study," Delaney said to me as we walked home that afternoon. The sun was shining, and the day was warm. So warm, in fact, that I didn't need my coat. I carried it under my arm as we walked, and the pleasant, fall sun felt gloriously warm after the recent cold days we'd had.

"That would be great," I replied.

"I'll go home and drop my stuff off. See you in about an hour?"

"Perfect," I said.

An hour later, I was seated alone at our dining room table. Dad was still at work; he wouldn't be home for several hours.

Time passed.

Delaney didn't show up.

Finally, I called her house. I figured that maybe she just got busy at home and wasn't going to be able to make it after all.

"Delaney?" her mom said. "Why, no, she's not here. She left quite a while ago on her bicycle, saying she was on her way to your house. She's not there?"

A sick feeling nibbled at the pit of my stomach.

"I'm sure she's on her way," I said to her mom. "She probably met a friend along the way and stopped to talk."

"You're probably right," Delaney's mom said. "But have her give me a quick call when she gets there to let me know she's arrived."

I promised I would, but as I hung up the phone, that sick feeling continued to eat away inside.

I looked at the clock. *Delaney should have been*

here forty-five minutes ago, I thought. *Riding her bike, it shouldn't take her more than five minutes to get here.*

One thing I wasn't going to do: I wasn't going to wait any longer. If Delaney was in trouble, every second would count.

But what kind of trouble could she get into? What could possibly have happened?

Deep down, I knew. I didn't want to think about it, didn't want to acknowledge it.

But I *knew.* It was only one word, and I wasn't going to admit I was even *thinking* about it.

I hurried to the side-by-side, put on my helmet, fastened my seat belt, and fired up the machine. In seconds, I was tearing down our two-track driveway, knobby tires spitting colorful leaves behind me.

Dogman.

No.

He's real. He's in the woods.

No.

He's waiting—

No!

And he was waiting for Delaney when she—

Stop thinking that!

I raced along the driveway, stopping at the road to make sure no cars were coming. I crossed the road to another trail that wound through the woods, a trail that looped back around and passed behind Delaney's house. It's the trail she would have taken to get to my house, and I was sure—

Hoping?

—I would find her.

I hoped.

Branches slapped at the machine as I navigated turns and raced over small hills and shallow ruts.

Delaney wasn't on the trail, and when I arrived at her house, she wasn't there. Something awful had happened, and I had a good idea what it was.

Delaney's mom was surprised to see me. When she opened the door and I told her that there was still no sign of her daughter, she gasped and turned, rushing across the living room.

"I'll call the police," she said, and she reached for the phone. Things were bad already, and I knew, now that the police would be involved, things were going to get much, much worse.

20

Just as Delaney's mom grabbed the phone, it rang. Without even looking at the caller ID on the handset, she answered, pressing the receiver to her ear.

"Hello?" she said. The word was quick, and I could hear the tension in her voice. Then, the sudden relief in her face told me everything I needed to know.

"You're *where?* At the *library?*" She paused, listening. "Jackson is here. You should have called earlier. We were worried sick. I was just about to call the police!"

The conversation didn't last long. Delaney's mom finally hung up the phone and gave me a weak smile.

"She'll be right here," she said. "She told me to tell you not to go anywhere. She said she found out some information about Dogman."

"At the library?" I asked.

Mrs. Granger nodded. "That's what she said. She said she found out a bunch of things there. She sounded pretty excited. Would you like some lemonade while you wait?"

I did, and I sat on their couch and sipped while I waited for Delaney. Before I finished the drink, she burst through the door, surprising both her mother and myself.

"He's really real!" she said, waving a handful of papers. "It's right here! I made copies!"

"Copies of what?" I asked.

For the next hour, Delaney and I went over the papers she'd copied at the library. Mostly, they were old newspaper clippings, stories of Dogman sightings, and even a few blurry photos. What she'd found was fascinating.

"You know," Delaney's mom said to us as she

came into the dining room. We'd spread the papers across the table, and it was completely covered. "That story was going around when I was a little girl growing up in Reed City, in the Lower Peninsula. We heard all sorts of crazy stories about Dogman."

"Were any of them true?" Delaney asked.

Her mother shrugged. "Who knows?" she replied. "Mostly, they were just fun stories to tell around the campfire. I don't think any of us gave any thought to the idea that they might be true. But I remember being scared out of my mind a few times. When I was eight or nine, there were more than a few times I had to spend the night in my parents' bedroom. I kept having nightmares about Dogman."

Delaney's mom left the dining room.

"Oh!" I said, nearly shouting. "I almost forgot to tell you about the scratches!"

Lines appeared on Delaney's forehead as she frowned.

"Scratches?"

"Yeah," I said. "When I went to check on Hops this morning, there were deep scratches on the shed door. Whatever made them was big, and I don't think it was a bear."

"Can I see?" Delaney asked.

I glanced at the clock. "Up to you," I asked. "What time do you have dinner?"

"When I get back from your house," Delaney said smartly. Then, she turned and called out: "Mom! Can I go over to Jackson's house? I'll be home around midnight!"

Midnight?!?! I thought.

"Absolutely not!" her mother hollered back from another room in the house. "It's a school night!"

"Can I go for an hour? I can make dinner for myself when I get back."

"That's more like it," her mother called back. "There's some of last night's chicken in the fridge."

Delaney smiled. "Works every time," she said with a wink.

Five minutes later, we were in the side-by-side, bouncing over ruts and bumps, winding along the trail that made its way through the forest, across Townline Road, and to my house. And all the while, it never occurred to us that, at that very moment, something might have been watching us from the forest.

21

The sleep was needed, and now the beast was hungry. He'd been up a good portion of the night, hunting, and around noon, he'd found a place deep in the woods where a tree had recently fallen, creating a place where he could hide, a place to curl up and sleep for a few hours. Now, he was awake again, alert, and moving.

And *hungry*. Always, it seemed, he was hungry.

But he liked his new home. His life on Drummond Island was much easier than his old life on the Lower Peninsula. There were fewer distractions and interruptions on the island, fewer noisy machines, and fewer people. Of course, having fewer people made his hunting a bit more challenging, but as in the past, he could survive on many types of food. Drummond Island offered various forms of food, with miles and miles of unspoiled wilderness, places to hide, to be alone, undisturbed and unchallenged.

And when a human happened by, and the time was right?

Well, then.

He moved slowly on all fours. If anyone had spotted him at a distance, they would have thought he was a very large deer, or maybe even a moose. A closer inspection would have revealed his canine, wolf-like appearance.

But no, not a wolf. He was bigger than a wolf. And more dangerous. More dangerous because he had not only the cunning and instinct of a predatory animal, but the thinking capability of a human.

Part dog.

Part man.

Dogman.

Throughout the afternoon, he stalked near the

highway, remaining hidden within the shadows of the colorful autumn leaves. Only once did he venture out to the road, when he'd picked up the scent of a deer and spotted the animal dead on the shoulder of the highway. The animal had recently been hit by a car . . . .

His hunger satisfied for the time being, the creature returned to the forest to rest.

But not for long.

He was disturbed by the noise of a machine, roaring through the forest, louder, closer.

The creature slunk back into the shadows as the noisy, smelly machine passed by on a trail. It contained two small humans, and the beast picked up their scent, even through the noxious fumes of burning gasoline and oil.

But he did not follow. Not this time. He would wait. Time was on his side. It was always on his side. In the wilderness, in the cover of the forest and the shadows of night, he was Ruler. He was King. He was smarter, craftier, stealthier, and stronger than any human could possibly be. He could remain in the distance and watch without being seen himself, could hunt without his prey even aware of him nearby.

Yes, time was on his side. And as the noisy, smelly machine passed by, he decided he would wait. This time.

22

The next day at school, it seemed like everyone was talking about Dogman. Of course, since there are only about fifty kids in the entire school, that's not very many. But as we were learning, other kids were hearing about or experiencing strange things.

The night before, I'd shown Delaney the scratches on the shed door. She was puzzled, and even a bit afraid. I told her that I didn't think the scratches were from a bear, but they could have been a wolf. But we both knew better.

"My dad says he saw something big on Johnswood Road last night," one kid said. "He said there was a big wolf snooping around a dead deer on the shoulder of the road. When he got closer, the wolf took off."

"That wasn't a wolf," another kid said. "That was Dogman."

"My uncle says that Dogman attacked him last week," a girl said. "And my uncle never lies."

I rolled my eyes and didn't say anything. The girl who had spoken was the same girl who claimed her uncle had been abducted by Bigfoot last summer. The summer before that, he'd claimed an alien spaceship had landed in his yard.

And that's how the stories went. Nobody had any real proof, nothing that would remove any doubt that Dogman was stalking the island. Nobody had any pictures or videos, only farfetched stories that were, at best, secondhand.

Still, I think everyone would agree that a dark shroud had fallen over the island. It was as though the community of Drummond Island was under the spell of a sinister shadow, some unseen, unknowable force that had scooped up the island in its powerful hand, slowly closing its fist on us, the inhabitants.

But the hardest part was separating fact from fiction. What was true and what wasn't? Even the articles and the pictures Delaney had copied at the library weren't proof. After all: people make up stories all the time, and the journalists report only what they're told. They don't send out a team of investigators every time there's a wild report or a crazy story reported by some backwoods farmer or an old woman with an overactive imagination. That would spoil all the fun. The stories were much better if simply reported, and let the reading public form their own conclusions.

But as for *my* conclusion? I wasn't sure. I had no idea if there was some half-dog, half-man creature living on the island, watching us from the shadows. I guess it seemed possible, but my common sense and appeal to reason told me that, most likely, there was another explanation.

A wolf?

Probably. That was the best, and most logical, explanation. It seemed to make the most sense.

Wolves are real.

Half-dog, half-man creatures *aren't.*

Or so it would *seem*.

Still, there was something else to consider. You can call it intuition; you can call it instinct. Or a gut feeling. Call it whatever you want, but something, somewhere, was telling me that there was more to this story than I was understanding. Something was telling me, whispering to me. Something told me to be on guard, to be watchful, especially when I ventured into the woods. I tried to push this feeling away, tried to tell myself that it was silly, that it was just my imagination.

It wasn't.

And that weekend, my darkest fears, the very worst parts of my imagination, would make a horrifying leap into reality.

23

Two days passed, and the creature had not had a hearty, solid meal. His instinct kept him cautious, and he'd had to settle for small scraps of food here and there, things he'd been able to scrounge, easy things he hadn't had to hunt. His hunger had grown to monstrous proportions and would be satisfied only by a nice, large, filling meal.

It was early evening. In the past couple of days, he'd stretched his territory. He spent time skirting the golf course before traveling north and skulking the shadows of several resorts near Scott Bay. One time he came close to being spotted by a man in the woods carrying a firearm. Even at a distance, he could smell the danger, the metal and gunpowder of a recent discharge, and he knew best to stay far, far away.

Now, as he looped his way back, he spotted yet another human.

A woman.

And a small dog.

Alone, on a desolate stretch of East Channel Road.

He sniffed the air and took in the scent of the woman and the little dog.

Nothing else.

No noisy machines were in sight; none could be heard or smelled.

A blob of drool formed on his lips.

And Dogman, hiding in the shadows of the forest, began to follow.

24

The woman didn't know why she was nervous. She'd started out on her walk with Binky, her little beagle mix, only minutes before, planning to walk along East Channel Road until she reached Sturgeon Bay Road, at which point she would turn around and head back. It was a walk she and Binky had made many times, especially during the fall months when the colors of the leaves were most vibrant. She and the dog enjoyed these walks, and she'd always felt safe, secure, never concerned about anything. And she certainly wasn't worried about any of the various animals she might encounter: raccoons, foxes, coyotes, deer, and, on rare occasions, a black bear. Last year she'd been fortunate enough to see a mother black bear and two cubs crossing the highway only a few hundred feet in front of her. She'd stopped walking and tightly clutched Binky's leash. Binky, for his part, barked once at the distant animals. The three bears paused and turned, glanced casually at the woman and the dog, and then continued ambling across the highway. After a moment, the woman continued her walk, and Binky went back to more important things like sniffing rocks and snapping at butterflies.

But now, as she walked along the familiar stretch of highway, she was very nervous. She turned and looked behind her, only to see empty road. Ahead of her was the same. And lining both sides of the road was nothing but thick trees, displaying a crayon box of colored leaves.

You're just being silly, she told herself, and she smiled and shook her head. *Nothing to worry about here.*

Binky stopped. His tail stiffened, and he lifted his left front paw and held it. His ears raised, and then he looked into the woods.

The woman stopped. She and the dog stared into the forest.

Again, she felt overwhelmed by the sensation that something was wrong. Was she being watched? She didn't see anyone or anything.

The sun dipped behind a cloud.

The little dog growled softly and remained motionless, rigid and tense. The woman tightened her grip on the leash.

What was that? she thought. *Did something move over there, in the woods?*

"Come on, Binky," she said softly. "Let's go back."

She turned around to head back, but stopped. This time, she *did* hear something in the forest. She was sure of it.

Farther up the road, she saw the shape of a car in the distance.

Binky, still staring off into the woods, growled louder. He started to whimper.

And the woman was afraid.

She started walking again, moving quickly. She'd never had this feeling before. Even though she tried to tell herself that she was just being silly, that there was nothing wrong, she couldn't shake the feeling.

So, she continued walking, faster, faster . . . .

25

From his hiding place in the shadows, the beast watched the woman and the little dog. The scent of both the human and the canine was strong, but there was another aroma that snared his attention: fear. To the creature, it was a fragrance, a sweet, delicious smell that was enticing and alluring. He could sense and smell fear in the wind, carried to his nose on the autumn breeze.

But he waited. He was cautious. The sun was high in the sky, and although the human and the dog were alone, he knew he'd be taking a risk by leaving the safety of the shadowy forest, in clear view. True, there was nowhere for the woman to run, and he knew he could quickly and easily overtake her.

And the dog? The dog was too small to create anything more than an annoyance.

The beast's nostrils flared. His heart rate climbed; his hair stiffened. His muscles tensed.

He was readying for the attack.

His eyes darted from side to side, up and down both sides of the highway. However, from his hiding place, much of his vision was obscured by branches and foliage. If he was going to make his move, he was going to have to do it now.

Lunge.

Attack.

Return to the shadows, to the safety of the forest.

He was ready. The time had arrived.

Dogman slowly rose on his haunches, standing firmly on his hind legs. He was over seven feet tall. He had not changed, but on his hind legs, he now had a more human-like appearance to him. If anyone were to see him now, they would argue that he might be a werewolf.

But no.

Not a werewolf.

He was much worse than that.

Much, *much* worse.

He sniffed the air one last time . . . .

26

The woman was nearly running now. Her steps were quick, and her pace was frantic. Her face was knotted with tension. Beside her, at her feet, Binky trotted along. All the while, the dog kept glancing into the woods and growling, tugging at his leash.

Up ahead, on the highway, the car drew nearer. The approaching vehicle gave the woman a bit of relief from the onslaught of fear that had suddenly stricken and nearly overtaken her.

She heard a branch snap in the forest.

Binky growled and barked.

The car approached.

The woman burst into a panicked run toward the vehicle. Gravel crunched beneath her feet.

Binky's full attention was now focused on the noise in the forest, and he had turned and was pulling at his leash, growling and barking.

The car approached, slowed.

With great relief, the woman recognized the man behind the wheel. She waved; the car rolled to a stop on the shoulder. She frantically threw the passenger door open and climbed inside, pulling Binky with her. She closed the door.

The car began to move, and drove on. Neither the driver nor his new passenger saw the dark figure at the edge of the woods, fuming with inhuman rage.

27

Saturday arrived in a burst of chilly air and a polished, blue sky. The leaves were frosted with a coating of dusty sugar, soon to dry as the temperature rose.

I was up early, and Dad was already gone. He had the day off work, but he'd told me that he was going to leave the island and drive to Newberry to help a friend fix a snowmobile and get it ready for winter. Most likely, he wasn't going to be home until evening.

As for me? I'd promised Delaney that I'd pick her up in the side-by-side and take her to see Lookout

Ledge. The place wasn't all that far away, but the trails to get there were winding and sharp, rolling up and down. The trails were a lot of fun to ride in the side-by-side, but there were many places where we'd have to go slow and take our time climbing up and around rocks and other obstructions.

"How far is it?" Delaney asked over the roaring of the engine.

"Not too far," I replied. "But we have to go slow in a lot of places. It shouldn't take us more than fifteen minutes or so to get there."

On the trail, there's a place on our property in a low-lying area that is always filled with water and mud. It's fun to ride through if you have a machine that is big and powerful enough. But our side-by-side would, most likely, get bogged down and waterlogged quickly. I'd never tried it before, and I wasn't going to try it today. So, we went around it, which required going very slow along the edge, crawling along over branches, saplings, and shrubbery.

Then, we bounced and jolted along the trail, winding though grassy, golden fields and tight-knit clusters of dark green pines and hardwoods until the path straightened out and went up a sharp hill that seemed to end in a wide, blue sky. At the very top, I halted and killed the engine, and our view expanded, panoramic and beautiful. In front of us and all around was a stunning portrait of green islands splashed with fall colors. Dark blue water met a light blue sky. Behind us, Drummond Island spread in a sea of dark green mixed with the fruit colors of fall. The terrain and trees were level in most places, but climbed up and down where hills and valleys lay. The richness and beauty in every direction was incredible.

The ledge itself, formed of coarse, gray limestone, was shaped like a jawbone, wide at the base and narrow at the tip. Millions of years of rain and wind had made the stone smooth. In fact, it was quite dangerous when it was wet, as the stone became very slippery.

And directly below and in front of the ledge: trees. Lookout Ledge was so high and dropped off so sharply that if we went any farther, we'd tumble down through the treetops before falling to our deaths some fifty or sixty feet below.

"Wow," Delaney said. "This is way cool. We're still on your property?"

I nodded. "Yep," I replied. "I don't think many

people know about this place, because the property has been in our family for years. In the summer, I ride out here all the time. We have it all to ourselves."

"How come you've never taken me here before?" Delaney questioned.

"You never asked," I said with a grin. "But there's another place I want to show you, too. We can take this trail out to Halfway Road. There's another trail that winds through a really cool swamp."

All the while, I'd never given any more thought to Dogman, to the stories circulating around school. Delaney and I didn't talk about the creature. I think we both realized that the stories and legends might be horrifying and scary, but that really was all they were: stories.

We were about to find out how wrong we were.

28

I turned the machine around, and we headed back down the steep trail, through dense forests, winding along and around hairpin turns as we made our way. As we entered a particularly dense portion of a thicket with soft earth, Delaney's arm suddenly shot out, pointing at the ground beneath the machine.

"Stop!" she cried.

I slammed on the brake pedal at the leading edge of a field, and the machine jerked to a violent halt. Our seat belts held us in place, but Delaney grabbed the side roll bar to hold on.

"What?" I asked.

"Look!" she said, continuing to point at the ground. "Tracks, like the ones we saw at the pond the other day!"

I looked. Sure enough, there were large, claw-like tracks in the soft earth. They crossed the trail we'd been riding on.

"Don't those look like the ones we saw at the pond?" Delaney asked.

I nodded, unbuckled my seat belt, and slipped out of the side-by-side. I knelt down to inspect the tracks, and Delaney joined me.

"These are fresh," I said, glancing up and looking around. "Look." I pointed. "Here's our tire tracks from when we came through just a little while ago. These animal tracks are made over top of our tire tracks. Whatever it was, it was here just a few minutes ago."

We looked around, our eyes scanning the thick forest around us. We saw nothing out of the ordinary. There was no movement, except the gentle swaying of tree branches, prodded by the gentle autumn breezes. However, there were plenty of places for an animal to hide. Animals tend to blend into their surroundings, and something could be watching us right now, staring at us, and we would never know it.

I stood and shut off the engine.

"What are you doing?" Delaney asked. I think she already had an idea, but she wanted clarification.

"Let's follow the tracks," I said.

"Are you out of your mind?!?!" Delaney said.

"We won't go very far. Let's just follow the tracks into the swamp. If we're quiet, maybe we can sneak up on whatever it is."

"And just what *is* it?" Delaney asked defiantly.

"My dad says it's probably a wolf," I said. "And if that's the case, we'll never see him. He'll be long gone by now. But just in case. Come on."

Reluctantly, Delaney stood. She took off her helmet and ran her hands through her long hair, unsnarling it and pulling it behind her head.

"Just for the record," she said, placing her hands on her hips, "I think this is a really, *really* bad idea."

And as it turned out, Delaney was right.

29

The tracks headed east. Because the ground was so soft, they created imprints that were easy to follow. I carefully looked at which direction they took and then looked up as I walked, searching for the animal.

"And what if it *is* a wolf?" Delaney asked. She was walking in my footsteps, just a few paces behind me.

"If that's the case," I replied, "the chances are we won't see him. Wolves are pretty crafty, and they like to stay away from humans when they can."

"But don't they attack humans?" Delaney asked.

I shook my head. "It's really rare," I replied. "They'd much prefer other prey like deer or smaller animals, animals that don't run fast or fight back. Nobody on Drummond has ever been threatened by a wolf, as far as I know."

"But there aren't many wolves on the island," Delaney said.

"Right."

"And what if these tracks don't belong to a wolf?" Delaney asked. "What if they belong to Dogman?"

Honestly, I'd been thinking the same thing. But my common sense kept insisting there was no such thing. All of the made-up stories were nothing more than that: made-up stories. Dogman was as real as Mother Goose and fairies and gargoyles and unicorns.

"I've been doing a lot of thinking about that," I said. "Seems like everyone is talking about Dogman at school and around town. But nobody has *seen* anything, really. I think you and I are the only ones who've seen tracks, and we don't know what kind of animal they belong to."

"What about the scratches on your shed?"

Delaney asked.

"Like Dad said: they were probably from a wolf. He probably smelled Hops and thought he'd be an easy meal. He didn't count on Hops being locked in his cage inside the shed."

I knew Delaney wasn't convinced, but, then again, neither was I. I wasn't sure I even believed myself.

But the idea of a real, live Dogman stalking Drummond Island—or anywhere in Michigan— seemed crazy, after I thought more about it.

I stopped walking to glance at the tracks near my feet. Here, away from the trail, the earth was firmer, and the tracks were more difficult to make out. But they were definitely fresh.

I looked up and all around, deep into the dense forest.

"Do you see anything?" Delaney asked.

I shook my head. "No," I replied.

But just because I didn't *see* something didn't mean I didn't *sense* something.

Once again, like that time at the pond, I had that creeping feeling that we were being watched.

"What is it?" Delaney said, dropping her voice.

"Shhh," I said.

I scanned the woods, slowly drawing my eyes over every inch of the forest around us. Growing up on the island, sharing the forest with so many wild animals, I always felt I was part of the environment, as though I was merely sharing space with the creatures of the woods.

But I didn't feel that way now. I felt as if we were intruders, as if we didn't belong.

And I didn't know why.

Suddenly, we heard a twig snap behind us. Delaney and I turned.

I felt Delaney's hand grab mine. She squeezed so tightly that I thought she was going to crush my fingers.

"Over there!" she hissed.

"Where?"

"There!"

And then I saw him.

I didn't say anything. The only thing I could do was stare directly ahead.

Peering at us from the forest was a creature unlike anything I'd ever seen before. An enormous, hulking dog with ratty, dark fur and sharp, pointed ears. His shoulders were broad and rounded, his neck was thick, and his muzzle was big and wide. His mouth was open, and his tongue hung out, and even from a distance, we could see rows of teeth, designed to rip bones and flesh to shreds.

And his *eyes*.

They were deep and dark, narrowed and piercing. If his eyes were razors, they would have cut us even from a distance.

He was looking at us.

We were looking at him.

It was then that I realized our huge mistake.

We have been following him, I thought. *We've been following his tracks. But all this time, he's been stalking us. It was as if he planned it this way, as if he knew we would see his tracks and follow. And now he has us where he wants us.*

"Oh, my gosh," Delaney said, in a voice just above a whisper. *"Is . . . is that a wolf?"*

Her answer came in the next moment, when the horrifying beast rose up on his powerful, hind legs . . . and began walking toward us.

30

As the beast slowly came toward us, the problem we faced became more and more real. By following behind us, he'd placed himself in the return path to the side-by-side. We couldn't even run in the direction of the vehicle, because we would be running right toward the beast. Our only chance would be to run in the other direction, but even then I knew that we'd never be able to outpace the animal.

But is that what he is? I wondered. *Is he an animal, or human? Both? Is he some sort of weird, hybrid werewolf?*

I had no idea. The stories and legends I'd heard about Dogman never really gave an indication as to where he'd come from or how he came to be.

My head snapped around. About twenty feet away was a maple tree. Thick branches grew low to the ground.

It was our only chance.

"Come on!" I yelled, and it was my turn to squeeze Delaney's hand. I pulled her for a moment and then released her hand as we both started to run.

"The tree!" I shouted as we sprinted. *"We've got to climb the tree! It's the only chance we have!"*

I never turned around to see how fast the creature was moving; I didn't dare. That would waste valuable time, time we needed to get to the tree. Every second counted, every moment mattered.

We reached the trunk. I spun quickly and grabbed Delaney around the waist, using every ounce of strength I had to help her up to the first branch. She grabbed the limb with both hands, and I let go. Then, I grabbed the same branch.

"Pull!" I shouted. "Climb as fast as you can!"

Behind us, I heard branches snap and twigs

break.

Like monkeys, our arms and legs wrapped around branches as we frantically hoisted ourselves higher and higher into the tree, farther and farther from the ground and the attacking beast.

A loud snarl came from below, much closer than I'd expected. I waited to feel sharp claws dig into my leg, to yank me from the tree and pull me to the ground, but the pain never came. I continued to climb. Delaney was a branch ahead of me, higher up.

At least one of us won't get eaten, I thought.

There was another snarl from below, this time louder, angrier. When I *did* manage to look down, I saw the creature on his hind legs, reaching up with powerful arms, or paws, or whatever they were. They looked like both.

One thing I was sure happy to see: he couldn't climb. He tried, but it didn't seem like he was able to get hold of any branches, at least not enough to give him enough grip to pull himself up.

"Keep climbing!" I shouted.

"Is he coming up the tree?!?!" Delaney shouted back.

"No, he can't get hold of the branches!" I

replied. "But keep going!"

We climbed a few more branches, a few more feet. Finally, I paused and looked down.

Dogman—because that's what he was, I knew that for sure—was at the base of the tree, directly below us. He'd given up trying to climb. He stood on his hind legs, reaching up with his hairy paws, as if to catch us.

Oh, man, I thought. *I hope these branches don't break. If a branch breaks and one of us falls—*

I didn't want to think about it.

"What do we do now?" Delaney asked.

"There's nothing we *can* do," I said. "We're just going to have to wait. We're safe in the tree, as long as we don't fall."

"But how long are we going to have to wait?" asked Delaney.

"However long it takes," I replied. "Like I said: there's nothing else we can do."

So, that's what we did. We waited. We held the branches and remained where we were, twenty feet off the ground. We were alive . . . and, at least for the time being, that was all that mattered.

31

Time seemed to drag on and on. Ten minutes seemed like an hour. Beneath us, the half-man, half-dog creature had given up attempting to climb the tree. Instead, he simply stood near the trunk on his hind legs, looking up, waiting for one of us to fall into his arms like an overripe fruit dropping from a branch.

"I wonder how long he's going to stay down there," Delaney said. "We can't stay up here forever. Sooner or later, someone is going to come looking for us."

And that was another thing that worried me. Delaney was right: if we were forced to stay in the tree all day, someone—my dad, Delaney's parents, maybe the police, too—would come searching for us. If Dogman was still hanging around, that would put other people at risk.

"I'll bet he goes away on his own," I said hopefully. "He's going to realize we aren't coming down, and he'll go find someone else to eat."

"That's comforting," Delaney said.

"Well, I don't know what he's going to do. But I *do* know that nobody on the island has been eaten by him. That would be big news, and it's never happened."

"Maybe he just got here," Delaney said. "Maybe there is a Mrs. Dogman and little Dogkids somewhere, vacationing on the island. Maybe they sent him out to bring back dinner."

I nearly laughed out loud. Delaney was being funny at a moment that wasn't very funny at all, and I think we both needed the humor. Our lives were at stake, and Delaney's lighthearted joke was a nice break from the serious, heavy tension.

"I don't know how long he's been on the island,"

I said. "The only Dogman stories I've heard about are from the Lower Peninsula."

"But maybe there is more than one creature," Delaney mused. "Maybe there are a bunch of them, roaming the woods. Maybe they just stay out of sight and keep to themselves, because they're too smart to get caught."

That was a possibility, too. Up until that week, I'd never considered any of the Dogman stories I'd heard to be anything but fiction. But now that we were seeing one, a real, live Dogman, up close and very personal, my ideas about those stories changed. Dogman was very, very real, and the proof was only twenty feet below us.

Finally, unbelievably, Dogman began to look disinterested. He began glancing in different directions, looking around the forest. His focus was shifting, and he wasn't so concentrated on the two of us in the tree.

Suddenly, Dogman dropped to all fours. This was the first time he'd done this since he'd forced us up into the tree. With a loud snarl and a deep, guttural howl, he took off running, crashing through the woods, snapping twigs and branches until those sounds faded completely.

Dogman was gone. Or at the very least, he'd left us alone.

It took us a long time to get up the nerve to climb down the tree. We waited a full fifteen minutes to make sure the hairy beast didn't return. When we didn't hear or see any more sign of him, Delaney and I slowly descended to the ground, ready at a moment's notice to climb back up if Dogman appeared again.

"All we need to do is make it to the side-by-side," I said. I eyed the forest suspiciously, scanning for any sign of the creature. "If we can make it back to the machine, we'll be home free."

"And if we don't make it back to the side-by-side?" Delaney asked.

"We will," I said, dodging her question. "I promise."

Which was a silly thing to do: promise something that I wasn't sure I could make good on. But I wasn't going to stand there and consider options. The only thing I was sure of at the moment was that we were wasting time just standing there, at the trunk of the tree.

"Follow me," I said. "We'll run back to the side-by-side. It shouldn't take more than a couple of minutes."

I started running through the forest, and Delaney followed closely behind. Every few seconds, I snapped my head around to make sure she was keeping up, but I was also looking behind us to make sure Dogman wasn't on our tail. I didn't know what we would do if he was, but if he was chasing us again, maybe we'd be able to climb a tree again and get away from him. That would be our only strategy, as there was no way we'd be able to outrun him. And certainly, there was no way we'd be able to fight him off. I think ten grown men would not be able to win a battle with Dogman.

It was a huge relief when the side-by-side came into view through the branches up ahead.

"Almost there!" I shouted.

In ten seconds, we were at the ORV. I leapt into the seat and quickly put on my helmet and seat belt. Delaney slipped into the seat next to me, and by the time she'd belted herself in and put on her helmet, I'd started the machine, put it into gear, and was roaring down the trail, headed for home. All we'd have to do is make it out of the forest, and we'd be safe.

But it wasn't going to be that simple.

32

We tore down the trail in the side-by-side, spewing a cyclone of leaves behind us. Every second that ticked by made me more and more relieved. It wouldn't be long, and we'd be out of the forest. I wasn't sure what we would do then, but the most important thing of all would be that we were *safe*. We were *alive*.

Of course, we'd have to go to the police. That would, most likely, be one of the first things we would do. I didn't know what would happen after that, but no one on Drummond Island was safe . . . not as long as that hairy monster was running around in the woods.

"Nobody's going to believe us," Delaney shouted over the roaring engine.

"Yes, they will," I shouted back. "You and I were *both* there. We have the same story. And besides: it won't be long before that thing makes another appearance. Someone else will see him, too."

"Let's just hope people believe us before it's too late," Delaney said. "Before that thing—"

Delaney's sentence was cut short by her scream, and I slammed on the brakes.

Ahead of us, on the trail, stood Dogman. He was on his hind legs, leering at us, his mouth open, fangs exposed, tongue lolling to one side.

And he was *enormous.* Gigantic. On his hind legs, he must've stood seven feet tall.

We sat in the idling machine, hearts pounding. Neither Delaney nor I said a word. We didn't move. The two of us stared at the beast, while he stared at us.

Finally, I spoke.

"Okay," I said quietly. "Hang on tight."

"What are you going to do?" Delaney asked.

"Just hang on, and don't let go. Your seat belt will keep you in, but you'll need to grab the bar to keep from being tossed around. Ready?"

With her right hand, Delaney grabbed the roll bar above her head.

"Yes, but what—"

Without waiting for Delaney to finish her sentence, I slammed my right foot on the accelerator. The machine lunged forward, spewing dirt and leaves and debris behind us . . . as I steered the side-by-side directly at the beast on the trail.

33

"What are you doing?!?!" Delaney shrieked as the side-by-side picked up speed.

"Just hang on!" I shouted back.

"You're going to run right into him!"

"Just hang on!"

I kept my foot on the accelerator, holding it to the floor. The engine roared, and we picked up speed. Faster.

"You're crazy, Jackson! You are out of your mind, completely crazy! Turn around!"

Faster . . . .

"Just hang on!"

Faster . . . .

"Jackson!"

The side-by-side flew down the trail, bouncing and jolting as the machine hit ruts and bumps. Dogman remained where he was, standing on his hind legs, staring us down, ready to hold his ground like a monstrous football linebacker.

Honestly, I had no idea if my plan would work. But the frame of the side-by-side is made of tubular steel, built to withstand some pretty harsh stuff. I was hoping—*hoping*—that we would be able to ram the beast, knock him over, and keep on going. I knew that if I'd taken the time to turn the ORV around and head the other way, Dogman would have easily caught up to us. At least by heading *at* the creature, by trying to drive into him and keep going, we would have a chance.

That was what I was betting on, anyway.

"Hold on!" I shouted one last time. Delaney, however, let go of the roll bar and covered her face with her hands.

I gripped the wheel tightly, held the accelerator

to the floor with my foot, and pushed myself back into the seat, bracing for the impact—

—that never came.

At the very last second, the enormous beast leapt to the side. We missed hitting him by mere inches. I never let off the accelerator, and we never slowed.

Even better! I thought, looking ahead at the open field. The trail was smoother here, and we could travel faster. Hopefully, we could put some distance between us and Dogman.

"It worked!" I shouted. *"I knew it would! I knew it!"*

"I can't believe you just did that!" Delaney screeched as she pulled her hands away from her face. She snapped her head around. *"But now he's coming after us! Fast!"*

34

I turned my head and saw the beast behind us. He was on all four legs now, running, no doubt much faster in this position.

I hadn't thought of that. I was thinking that he would be running on *two* legs, like a man. I hadn't counted on him using all *four.*

"We'll make it," I assured Delaney, although I wasn't so sure myself. I had no idea how fast the beast could run.

As we made our way across the field, we kept

our distance from him, which meant we were going about the same speed. But whenever I had to go around a rut or slow for a bump, I whipped my head around and saw Dogman gaining on us. There was no reason for him to slow down, and he kept coming like an ugly, three-hundred pound hairy rhino.

But up ahead, there was a wide open area that would provide the break we needed. The trail was straight, and the ground was flat and smooth. I wouldn't have to slow to go around any dips or bumps or big ruts.

If we can only make it . . . .

Dogman had decreased the space between us, and was now only a few dozen yards behind.

"He's catching up to us!" Delaney yelled.

"Not for long!" I shouted. "If we make it to that field up there, we can go full speed and leave him behind!"

It took only about ten seconds, but it felt like an hour. Finally, we reached the field where I could once again hold the accelerator to the floor, and we could fly. Top speed of the side-by-side was about sixty miles an hour, but I've never gone that fast. There's never been a need to. Side-by-sides are meant for off-road use, climbing hills and going places a regular vehicle can't go.

As we raced through the field, the side-by-side continued to pick up speed. The field ended, and trees flew past as we entered the forest again, but the trail remained smooth.

Behind us, there was no sign of Dogman. Oh, I was sure he was still coming after us, but we'd been able to put some distance between us and him.

And maybe, just maybe, he would give up the chase. I certainly hoped so.

However, up ahead, there was something I'd completely forgotten about: the low-lying area, the long stretch of trail filled with water and mud.

I steered around a sharp corner, only slowing a little. When the trail straightened, and I saw what was before us, it was already too late.

"Jackson! Stop!"

"I can't!" I shouted back. "We can't stop now! We'll have to try to plow through it!"

And suddenly, we'd plunged into the long patch of dirty, muddy water that sat like a narrow lake in the middle of the trail. The machine instantly bogged down and slowed, and I could feel the engine working to push through the water.

Slower, slower . . . .

"Come on, come on!" I shouted to the side-by-side, coaxing it on.

"Jackson!"

"Come on, make it through!" I was talking to the side-by-side at this point, as if the engine would listen to me, urging it on, to keep going, to push through . . . .

And we almost made it.

The machine bogged to a stop, just as we were nearing the end of the mud hole. Water rose above the floorboards, soaking our shoes and pant legs.

"Get out!" I shouted to Delaney. "We need to pull it out! If we can pull it to the side and get the tires out of the water and mud, we might be able to get some traction and keep going!"

We hastily unbuckled our seat belts and rolled out of the side-by-side. The water and mud were ice cold and went up past our knees.

"Grab the roll bar and pull!" I ordered.

However, very quickly we found that the machine wasn't going to budge. Not an inch.

"Jackson!" Delaney wailed. "Look!"

I turned around.

Dogman was coming. He was on his hind legs now, walking swiftly but cautiously, edging along the side of the long, muddy puddle.

Our off-road vehicle was stuck, buried in the mud.

We were stranded.

There was no way we could outrun Dogman.

There was nowhere we could go.

35

Think quick, Jackson, I told myself.

So, I did.

I leapt into the idling side-by-side, grabbed the wheel, and slammed my right foot down on the accelerator.

"Jackson!" Delaney screamed, but I didn't pay attention, and I didn't reply.

The machine moved. A little at first, and then it crawled forward. Relieved of Delaney's weight, the side-by-side was able to pull out of the mud pit.

Still moving slowly, I turned to see Delaney rushing through the muddy water toward me.

"Hurry!" I said. "Get in! We can still get away!"

"I thought you were going to leave me!" she shouted as she scrambled into the side-by-side. When she was seated, I hit the accelerator again, and the machine charged forward. Dogman was behind us. He was still on his hind legs, and he was still coming toward us, but we were no longer stuck in the mud. We had a fighting chance again.

"Okay, hang on," I said. "This might get a little rough."

"You mean it hasn't been bad enough already?!?!" Delaney asked.

I turned my head. Dogman had once again dropped to all fours, and he was running as fast as a deer.

I tried to remember all of the places along the trail where we could go fast or, at the very least, fast enough to outpace the racing beast. But I knew the woods and trails well . . . and I knew that Dogman had the advantage. We still had nearly a mile of trails to travel before we reached a main road. Dogman was sure to catch up to us by then.

Unless . . . .

"He's catching up again!" Delaney shouted.

"All right," I said. "I've got another idea."

I suddenly swung the side-by-side off the trail and steered it through a small growth of thin alder trees. We rolled over them easily and found another trail. I turned sharply to the left and then hit the accelerator.

"Where are we going?" Delaney shouted.

"Back up to Lookout Ledge!" I shouted back.

"But we'll have to go slow up the hill! That thing will catch us for sure!"

"That's what I'm hoping for!" I shouted back. Glancing behind me, I didn't see any sign of the pursuing beast. But I knew he was still after us.

"You're crazy!" Delaney shouted.

"You've already said that a billion times!" I shouted back. "Pretty soon, I'm going to start to believe it! Trust me! I know what I'm doing!"

"Are you sure?!?!"

No, I thought. *No, I'm not sure at all. Delaney's right: I'm crazy for trying this.*

But I also knew it was our only hope, our only chance of getting out of this thing alive. If my plan worked, we could finally go home. We would live another day.

But if my plan didn't work?

I shot a quick glance behind us.

Dogman was crashing through the brush, and he looked angrier than ever.

"Okay!" I shouted to Delaney. "Hang on, and be brave. This is where things are going to get tricky!"

36

The trail I'd cut to was a little-used hunting trail, frequented only during certain times of the year. But it merged with the main trail that led back to the place Dad and I called Lookout Ledge . . . and that's where my plan was either going to succeed or fail miserably.

And if it failed?

I couldn't think about that. I had to focus on success. I had to focus on winning. I had to know, deep down, that I would succeed. I didn't want to think about failure.

We merged onto the main trail. Here, the ground turned rocky and quickly rose in elevation. We'd have to go much slower at this part.

Delaney turned.

"He's getting closer, Jackson!" she shouted.

"I know, I know," I said. "That's what I want."

"You want—"

"Trust me on this!" I said loudly. "It's our only chance. But you have to do exactly as I say. Is your seat belt fastened tight?"

"Yes!"

"Good!"

"Keep watching behind us!" I shouted. "I can't always turn my head to look, because we're bouncing around so much. I need to know how close he is!"

"He's about five car lengths behind us!"

"Okay," I said, and I focused on the uphill trail ahead. My timing had to be perfect, or else I would—

No, I thought. *Don't think about that. This will work. This will work. This will work.*

I kept repeating that phrase over and over in my head as the side-by-side bounced and tossed back and forth, jolted by large rocks and deep ruts.

"Closer," Delaney said.

I sped up, giving us a little distance as we climbed the hill.

"How about now?" I asked loudly.

"Farther. Only a little."

We kept going. Other thoughts whirled through my mind, things like what would happen if we ran out of gas at that moment or if the machine stalled for some reason. Things like that happen in books and movies all the time. Just when you thought the main character was going to get away from the villain, he or she was faced with some other problem to overcome.

But thankfully, that didn't happen to us. The side-by-side, although caked with mud, continued to roar up the hill, as fast and powerful as ever.

"Where is he?" I asked.

"Catching up!" Delaney replied.

I continued driving the machine up the hill, pushing it over rocks and dips and bumps. The fat, knobby tires dug deep, giving great traction.

"He's getting closer!" Delaney yelled. I could hear the sheer panic and terror in her voice.

Lookout Ledge came into view, about twenty feet in front of us. Beyond, the only thing I could see were puffs of white clouds in a China blue sky.

"Jackson! He's right behind us! He's going to—"

I slammed the accelerator with my foot, and the side-by-side burst forward. Because we were headed up at such a sharp angle, there wasn't a very noticeable increase in speed.

Delaney screamed. The machine jolted and shook, and a shadow fell over us.

Dogman had leapt, attacking from behind. He'd jumped and landed on the roll bars of the side-by-side, and now he was riding on top, gripping the ORV with three paws. With the other, he reached down and wrapped it around Delaney's neck!

Once again, I was faced with something I hadn't planned on. And I had to admit, even though I didn't want to, that my plan, my last-ditch effort to save Delaney and I, had failed.

37

It took me a moment to realize that the high-pitched roaring of the engine wasn't the engine at all; it was Delaney. She was screaming at the top of her lungs, trying to pull the beast's arm from around her neck. Being strapped in by the seat belt made it all that more difficult for her.

Then, the creature itself let out a loud, deep snarl, a tribal roar that was as deep and dark and black as an endless pit. Delaney squirmed in her seat and crouched low. Somehow, she was able to wriggle free from Dogman's arm.

Which, of course, only made the animal angrier. He roared again and took a wild, mad swipe with his powerful paw. He missed Delaney but clipped my shoulder, tearing a hole in my sweatshirt.

"Do something!" Delaney wailed. She was leaning forward as far as she could, trying to stay beyond reach of the flailing paw with razor-sharp claws.

Ahead of us, the trail rose sharply, and I knew that, with the added weight of Dogman on top of the side-by-side, there was a very real danger of the vehicle becoming off-balance and flipping over backward.

So, I did the only thing I could do: I kept my foot on the accelerator, pressed to the floor, and steered the machine straight up, heading for Lookout Ledge.

Delaney saw the ledge looming closer, the sky above becoming wider and wider.

"Jackson!" she screamed. "What are you doing?!?! You're going to kill us!"

I said nothing. I was too focused. I had to be.

Once again, Dogman howled and took another

wild, powerful swipe with his paw, this time ripping into the seat. Delaney screamed again.

We were ten feet from the top of the ledge, the precipice of death. On the other side of the ledge, the sky opened wide and the terrain fell away. If we continued on at the speed and direction we were headed, the side-by-side and the three of us would be sent over the edge, into the air, crashing through the trees and to the ground a hundred feet below. None of us would survive.

But I wasn't quite ready to give up.

Delaney screamed again.

"Hang on tight!" I barked. *"Don't let go!"*

Dogman took another swipe with his paw and missed once again.

We were at the ledge.

At the very last moment before I knew we would go over, I cranked the steering wheel as hard as I could, turning the side-by-side to the left. I hit the brakes. Knobby tires grabbed loose gravel, grasping at traction that wasn't there. The vehicle slid sideways, off-balance.

Sliding . . . .

And Dogman was off-balance, too. The force of

the turn, the momentum of the ORV caused him to lose his grip.

Sliding—

The machine slid sideways and came to a sudden, jerky stop. The force of the stop caused the giant, hairy beast to lose his grip. He went flying off the top of the side-by-side, into the blue sky. Flailing his four paws madly, he suddenly vanished, over the ledge and out of our sight, plummeting down, down, into the trees and to the ground far below.

Delaney was strapped in her seat, head down, hands in her face. She was whimpering.

"We're all right," I said. "We're alive."

I killed the engine, and the idling ended. Now, the only thing we could hear was the cold wind whistling along the ledge, whispering at our ears.

I took a deep breath, unbuckled my seat belt, and climbed out. I lifted my helmet from my head and tucked it under my arm. Carefully, I walked around to the side of the ORV and looked down.

The tires were only inches from the ledge. If I hadn't turned and hit the brakes when I did . . . .

"Are . . . are we alive?" Delaney asked, and I laughed.

"That's a pretty silly question," I said. "Yes, we are. But I don't think Dogman is doing so well."

Delaney lifted her head and looked around. "Where is he?" she asked.

I pointed over the ledge. "Down there somewhere," I said.

Slowly, Delaney unbuckled her seat belt, removed her helmet, and got out of the side-by-side. She stood back from the ledge and looked at the skid marks left by the tires.

"We almost went over the cliff," she said.

"I know," I replied. "But I knew it was our only chance."

Delaney snapped her head around and looked at me.

"You . . . you mean you *planned* this to happen?"

"Sort of," I said. "I was hoping Dogman would chase us, and I would turn at the last moment, and he would go over the ledge. I hadn't planned on him actually jumping onto the side-by-side. But it all worked out. Not quite the way I'd imagined, but it worked out. He's dead. We're alive."

"Are you sure he's dead?" Delaney asked,

looking down through the thick trees below. I glanced into the distance, to the northwest, at the islands dotting the bay.

"Nothing could survive that fall," I replied.

Delaney looked up. "Your sweatshirt is ripped," she said.

I looked at my right shoulder. My sweatshirt had a six-inch slice across the top, but Dogman's swipe had missed my skin.

"I think I'll live," I said. "Come on. Let's go home."

38

Three days later.

The entire island community was abuzz with our Dogman story. Delaney and I were able to lead police and other people to the trail where Dogman's tracks were discovered. Trackers were able to find some of the creature's fur on branches, and it was sent to a lab somewhere in Michigan's Lower Peninsula for testing.

And there were other people who'd reported sightings, too. Some of them claimed they'd actually seen the beast earlier that week, but didn't tell anyone because they knew no one would believe them. Once Delaney and I came forward with our story, other people opened up.

But a mystery still remained: what happened to Dogman?

His body was never found. Dad, Delaney, and I, along with a dozen other searchers, scoured the forest beneath Lookout Ledge. We found nothing except a few long, scraggly, dark brown hairs. No blood, no tracks. Whatever had happened to Dogman was a mystery.

Many people came to search for the creature. A team of Bigfoot hunters arrived, and they interviewed Delaney and me several times. We tried to tell them that what we saw wasn't a bigfoot creature. We described in great detail everything we could remember and told them that the beast had been some sort of half-dog, half-man creature. Like a werewolf, but not quite.

"But that's silly because werewolves don't exist," said the guy who was leading the hunt for Bigfoot. None of those searchers found anything on their hunts, either.

Weeks passed. Everyone on the island was on edge, wondering if and when there would be another Dogman sighting. The half-eaten carcass of a deer was found in the woods by a hunter, but wolf tracks were found nearby, and they were much smaller than the footprints made by Dogman.

November gave way to December, and there were no reports of strange tracks in the snow.

Dogman had simply disappeared, vanishing into thin air . . . until February came.

39

Everyone on the island had advance warning of the coming blizzard, so we were prepared. Over fifteen inches of snow caused school to be cancelled for two days. Power was knocked out. Most of my friends spent the day helping with snow removal and riding snowmobiles. A blizzard on the island was more like a party atmosphere, if you ask me. I always laughed when I saw huge snowstorms strike big cities. They get six inches of snow, and everybody whines like it's the end of the world. For us in northern Michigan, especially on Drummond Island, snow time meant play time.

But reports soon came out on the local news that had nothing to do with the blizzard. A woman in DeTour Village, on the mainland of the Upper Peninsula, reported seeing what she called a 'giant dog' in her yard one night, during the snowstorm. The falling snow, however, filled in any tracks that would have been left.

Two days later, about twenty-five miles away in Cedarville, large tracks—the same size and shape left by Dogman on Drummond Island—were discovered near the harbor.

A day after that, near Pontchartrain Shores, a man photographed a dark figure near his barn. The picture was blurry, but it sure looked a lot like the beast that had attacked Delaney and me on the island. Tracks in the snow led across the ice to Mackinac Island. Although no one on the island reported seeing anything unusual, his tracks wound through the island and into the center of town. The tracks again crossed the ice, this time farther south, across the frozen Straits of Mackinac. In Mackinaw City, the tracks in the snow continued at Fort Michilimackinac State Park, which was closed for the season.

The beast—the horrifying, legendary creature known as Dogman—had returned to Michigan's Lower Peninsula.

And to this day, he's still out there, somewhere in the night, waiting and watching from the shadows in the darkness.

Waiting, watching.

Stalking.

40

Spring came.

It's a magical time of the year on Drummond Island. The ice and snow give way to rain and warmer temperatures. The leaves return to the trees, and everything is lush and green and full and rich. The spring and summer months have often been referred to as a 'rebirth' of sorts, with everything new and fresh. Nowhere is that more apparent and true than on beautiful Drummond Island.

Of course, summer followed tightly on spring's

departing heels. For me, that meant two things. First, it meant that school let out. I like school, for the most part, but by the time May and June rolled around, the only things on my mind were the summer months and all of the things I would do on the island. I know a lot of kids are into computers and video games, and I guess I like those things, too.

But I like being outside best of all. In the woods, hiking, fishing, exploring, riding the side-by-side . . . my summers on the island are like living in a waking dream, every day.

The only bad news was that Dad told me that there was a chance we were going to move to Sault Ste. Marie, in the Upper Peninsula of Michigan. He said that he might have to go there for work, and if so, we would be moving. I hoped not, because I would miss the island and my friends. But I didn't have to think about that for a while.

One afternoon in July, Delaney and I rode the side-by-side out to Turtle Ridge ORV Park, which is open from May through November. People come from all over with their four-wheel-drives, dirt bikes, and other off-road vehicles. There are miles and miles of trails and hills to ride, and it's one of the most popular tourist places on the island. Of course, there are lots of other things to see and do, but Turtle Ridge is my favorite. Delaney's too.

The day was sunny, and the place was busy! There were four-wheel drive vehicles lined up in the gravel parking lot, with many of them heading out or coming in from the trails.

"Lots of people today," Delaney said as I shut off the engine. We took off our helmets and stood, standing and stretching next to the side-by side. We gazed at some of the souped-up Jeeps and trucks and other vehicles parked all around. A long row of dirt bikes and four-wheelers, caked with mud, were parked nearby.

From behind us, I heard a girl's voice approaching.

"It's all made up," I heard her say.

"No, it's not," a boy's voice replied.

"There's no such thing as Dogman," the girl insisted.

That got our attention. Delaney and I looked at each other and then turned to see a boy and a girl about our age, walking toward us.

"It's all just a bunch of nonsense," the girl

continued. "My dad says so. Those kids that said Dogman attacked them last fall probably made everything up."

"No, we didn't," Delaney quickly shot back.

The boy and girl stopped in their tracks and looked at us.

"That was us," I chimed in. "We were the ones it happened to, and we didn't make up anything."

"Sure it did," the girl said, rolling her eyes.

"No, really," Delaney said. "It happened. Dogman is real."

The girl's name was Fern, and the boy was Liam. They were cousins, both from Lansing, Michigan. They were on vacation, a big family reunion of sorts. All of the people in their family, Fern told us, were huge off-road fans, so that's why they'd all gathered on Drummond Island.

Fern and Liam listened intently as we recounted the horrifying experience we'd had the previous fall. When we were finished, the two cousins looked at one another.

"Well," Fern said, "I still find it hard to believe. But you sound like you're telling us the truth."

"You can't make up stuff like that," Delaney

said. "Every word of what we said is true. And he's still out there, somewhere, most likely on the Lower Peninsula."

Fern and Liam looked at one another.

"Well," Fern said, "we've got a story that's even more horrifying than that."

Delaney and I looked at one another, puzzled.

"What could be more horrifying than a giant, hairy creature that wants to gobble you up?" she said.

"Leprechauns," Liam replied, as if just the word alone would back up Fern's claim.

I nearly laughed out loud, but I wanted to be polite.

"Leprechauns," I said. It was meant to be a question, but that's not the way it sounded.

Fern and Liam nodded.

"Exactly," Fern said. "But I'm not talking about fake leprechauns. Real ones. Scary ones."

Again, I suppressed the urge to laugh. Fern was out of her mind—and so was her cousin—if they expected us to believe anything about real leprechauns.

"Scary leprechauns?" I asked with a slight smirk and raised eyebrows. Even if leprechauns *were* real, I couldn't see anything scary about them.

Delaney, however, looked fascinated. "You aren't kidding?" she asked.

Fern and Liam shook their heads.

"I wish we were," Fern said. "Want to hear about it?"

Did we ever.

And so, we listened, just as intently as they had listened to our Dogman story, as Fern and Liam told us all about the Lair of the Lansing Leprechauns.

Next:

Johnathan Rand's

MICHIGAN
CHILLERS®

#20: Lair
of the
Lansing
Leprechauns

Continue on for
a FREE preview!

1

"Is it ever going to stop raining?" I asked.

"I'm sure it will soon enough, Fern," Mom said.

Her voice surprised me. I had thought I was alone in the living room—except for Bentley, our dog—and I had spoken the words out loud, thinking they would only be heard by myself. And Bentley, of course. But I flinched a little when I heard my mom speak. She had caught me off guard.

I turned. Mom was standing at the foot of the carpeted stairs, and I hadn't heard her come down.

187

"It seems like it's been raining forever," I continued. "I don't think it's ever going to stop, and I'd really like to go outside. I hate being stuck here in the house."

"I think I heard that it's supposed to end later today," Mom said, glancing at the phone in her hand. "And the sun is supposed to come out."

"I hope so," I said. "I'm going crazy."

Mom smiled. "Well, we sure need the rain," she said. "It's been a dry summer. It's about time we got a good, long storm. All of the plants were dry and dying. See how green the grass is now?"

I looked out the rain-streaked window. Mom was right, of course. It *had* been a dry summer. When the rain came, everyone seemed happy about it . . . but that was *days* ago.

"Yeah," I replied. "I know we need rain. But not *this* much."

Mom just laughed and made her way to the kitchen.

"I'll bet you'd like to go outside, too, huh boy?" I said, glancing at Bentley. Bentley is a brown and white boxer, mixed with a couple of different breeds. At least that's what our veterinarian says. We adopted him from the animal shelter last year, and he's become one of my very best friends.

Bentley lifted his chin from his front paws. He cocked his head and looked at me with his big, brown eyes, knowing I'd spoken to him, waiting to hear my next words. I swear that sometimes, Bentley can understand what I'm saying.

"You wanna go outside, too, don'tcha?" I said, kneeling down and patting him on the head. Bentley thumped his tail happily and licked my wrist.

"Don't worry," I continued. I gave him a quick hug, then stood. Again, he looked at me expectantly, wondering if we were going somewhere and what we were going to do.

I looked out the window again, wishing it would quit raining.

Two hours later, I got my wish.

The clouds broke into enormous white and gray puzzle pieces, changing shape as they drifted apart, allowing the backdrop of beautiful blue sky to peek through. It was still raining, but not quite as hard.

Blades of sun knifed through the clouds, shining on trees and making their leaves all glossy and bright, green and healthy.

And not far away:

A spectacular rainbow with vibrant, shimmering colors arced through the sky. The sight was mesmerizing, and I felt hypnotized by the simple, sheer beauty of the phenomena. All I could do was stare. The rainbow looked like it ended in a vacant field a few blocks away.

Suddenly, I had an idea.

There's supposed to be a pot of gold at the end of every rainbow, I thought. *At least, that's what I've always heard.*

Of course it wasn't true.

Of course it was silly.

Still—

"Wanna go find a pot of gold, Bentley?" I asked my dog.

Hearing his name and the question in my voice, Bentley stood. He stretched, then nuzzled my hand dangling at my side. I gave him a few quick scratches behind his ears. His big, loving eyes stared up at me.

I'm ready, Fern! Let's go! his eyes said. *I'm a good boy! I'm a good boy! Can I go, too, can I, can I, huh? Huh?*

I laughed, knelt down, and kissed his nose. If

you think that's gross, well, I guess you're just not a dog person.

"All right," I said, and I glanced out the window. The rainbow was still there, radiating brilliantly, but I knew it would be gone soon.

"Mom, I'm taking Bentley to find the pot of gold at the end of the rainbow!" I called out. "I think it's in the field!"

"Watch the time," Mom replied from the kitchen. "Be home for dinner."

I felt for my phone in my back pocket. "Okay," I said.

"And if you find any gold, bring some back for your father and I. We could use it to help pay for a few things around here."

"Ready to go?" I said to Bentley as I walked to the front door. His leash was dangling from a coat rack, and when he saw me grab it he rushed up to me and sat, shaking with excitement as I fastened the leash to his collar.

"Good boy," I said. "Let's go find that pot of gold!"

Of course, I knew we wouldn't find a pot of gold. That was just a legend, an old wives' tale. A myth. A make-believe story.

But there *was* something waiting for us at the end of the rainbow: the beginning of a nightmare.

2

Water puddled on the streets and the sidewalk. Wet grass glistened in the sun. Everything was bright green and lush and beautiful. The air was warm and smelled fresh and new, as if the storm had scrubbed the neighborhood clean. The sun was shining, most of the clouds had fled, and it was a gorgeous day. It was hard to imagine that, only hours before, rain had been falling in sheets and buckets from a dark, gray sky.

And in the distance, the rainbow was still there, gleaming and shining. I knew it wouldn't be long before it was gone. I wondered how many other people in Lansing had spotted it. That's where we live, of course. Lansing is a city in Michigan's lower peninsula and it's probably known best for being the state capital. The city is located toward the lower middle part of the state, about half way between Grand Rapids to the west and Detroit to the east.

Not far from our home is the Capitol building. That's where all of the Michigan legislators and lawmakers work, including the governor. There are a lot of other people who work there, too. So, as far as cities, go, Lansing is a pretty important place.

Bentley was still sniffing a bush, and I tugged gently at his leash, pulling him away.

"Come on, Bentley," I said. "We have more important things to find."

We crossed the street and strode along the sidewalk. Earlier in the year, my friends and I had created colorful designs on the concrete using chalk. Over the summer our creations had faded, and now only blotchy blobs remained, distorted and misshapen by the rain.

I glanced up. The rainbow was fading, but it was still there. It arced high in the sky, one end of it still stretching down into the distant, empty meadow not far from our home. Except now, the end of it appeared to be obscured by a small forest at the edge of the field.

Soon, Bentley and I were wading through tall, knee-high grass. After only a few steps my shoes and pant legs were soaked, but I didn't mind. I hardly paid attention, anyway, because I was too focused on the rainbow in the sky. I had thought that, by now, it would have faded away. The sun was shining, of course—that helped created the rainbow—but it also must be raining, which is how rainbows are made. The sun shining on the falling rain created a prism effect, causing the beautiful band of colors I was now seeing.

And the rainbow's end was still right in the middle of a clump of trees at the edge of the field.

"The rainbow is still there," I said to Bentley. "That's odd.

Although I had set out in search of the end of the rainbow to find the mythical pot of gold, I really didn't believe I'd find anything. In fact, I knew I wouldn't find the end of the rainbow. I was just looking for something to do after being cooped up in the house for so many days and not being able to go outside.

I could hear the sounds of the city in the distance: the hum of tires on pavement, a car horn here and there. A small airplane in the sky.

And closer, I could hear droplets of water falling from the trees, making gentle smacking sounds as they hit leaves.

Bentley stood rigid and stiff, staring into the woods. In the sky, the end of the rainbow fell into the canopy of trees and vanished.

"Ready to find some gold?" I asked Bentley with a laugh. Bentley glanced at me and wagged his tail, then returned his gaze to the forest. He seemed intensely interested in something, focused and attentive, on guard.

"What is it, buddy? See a bunny rabbit?" I asked.

I started walking ahead, into the forest. Reluctantly, Bentley came along at my heels. I'd been in the field dozens of times, but I'd never ventured into the small gathering of trees on the far side, where I was at the moment. The field was a place where my friends and I played during the summer months, but we didn't really have cause to venture far to the other side where the trees grew.

There wasn't a trail to follow, but I wasn't concerned about getting lost. I knew that the forest was very small, and we were so close to the edge of the field, which bordered another neighborhood on the other side.

Bentley stopped walking and started growling softly. I, too, stopped walking, alarmed by the warning in Bentley's growl. Dogs have intuition and instinct that humans don't, and can see and hear things we can't.

"What do you see?" I whispered.

Bentley shot me a quick glance, then returned his gaze to the woods.

I turned in the direction he was looking, but I didn't see or hear anything different or strange. And it was unlikely that there was someone else in the woods. I knew none of my friends would be here, not now, not when it had been raining only a short time ago.

Bentley and I were alone.

Or, that's what I thought at that moment.

Then, I took a few more steps, and made a discovery that would turn my world upside down and inside out.

3

When I took a few steps forward, Bentley hadn't followed. He stood his ground until the leash became taut. I turned.

"What's the matter?" I asked, and yes, I did expect him to answer. Not in any human way, not with some sort of voice or anything. But I knew my dog well enough to know that he could communicate in his own way, and I was sure he could understand at least the intent of my words if not their meaning.

Bentley wagged his tail a few times, glancing at me, then back at the forest.

"There's nothing there," I said. "Come."

Reluctantly, Bentley stopped growling and followed.

One step.

Two.

Three.

Four.

Five—

I stopped walking.

Bentley stopped.

What in the world? I thought.

I blinked my eyes several times, but nothing changed.

Ahead of us, partially obscured by trees, were blue mushrooms of enormous size. Not only that, but they were glowing, shimmering like neon lights.

Again, I blinked my eyes, thinking that I was seeing things. Or maybe it was my mind playing

199

tricks on me.

Nope. The mushrooms were still there, tall and blue.

Glowing.

Bentley began growling softly again, but it wasn't a mean growl. It was a growl of gentle warning, but curiosity, too. He was leaning forward, caught by his own desire to flee and his urge to move ahead, to explore this strange mystery we were both seeing.

Water dripped from trees, and a few droplets landed on my head. One landed on my cheek, I and wiped it away.

I took another step, then another. Bentley, attached to his leash, had no choice but to come with me.

Mushrooms—giant, blue, glowing—towered above us, as tall as a one-story house. I counted eight of them. They were all about the same size, and their stems growing up from the ground were at least two feet in diameter, bigger than some tree trunks.

What I was seeing, I knew, was impossible. While I haven't been all over the world, I knew enough that no mushroom on Earth grew to this size.

And yet, here they were, eight of them in all, tall and blue and glowing as if electricity were running through them.

I stood in shocked amazement, marveling at the mysterious discovery, already knowing what my mom and dad would say.

Suddenly, I remembered my phone in my back pocket. I pulled it out and turned it on, swiped to the camera app, and clicked off a few pictures. In the tiny glass window, the frozen images were crisp and clear.

There! I thought. *Proof! Now I have proof to show people!*

I took a few more pictures, then I had another idea. Closing out the camera app, I quickly speed-dialed mom, but the call wouldn't go through. I looked at the signal indicator, and only one bar was lit. I tried calling again, but the same thing happened.

I quickly composed a text. Usually, a text will go through when a call won't.

`At the field! Found giant mushrooms!`

I hit the send button.

Whoosh.

I waited.

Ding!

`That's nice.`

My fingers tapped quickly.

`I'm serious!`

Send.

Whoosh.

Waited.

Ding!

`Don't eat any of them. Some mushrooms are poisonous.`

I swiped through my image library and found one of the pictures of the mushrooms. I tried sending it to mom, but it failed. Tried again. Failed. And again.

"Ug," I said out loud, and Bentley looked at me. He wagged his tail.

"I can't get this picture to go through,

Bentley," I said.

Bentley nudged my knee with his nose, and then he quickly snapped his head sideways, alerted by something he saw or heard. He stood motionless, growling softly.

"What?" I asked. "What do you—"

I stopped speaking when I heard a noise.

Or, rather, a *voice.*

A thin, tiny voice, not far away. It stopped suddenly, as if whoever was speaking was suddenly aware that someone had heard them.

Bentley continued to growl softly.

"Shush," I said quietly.

I looked around and up, still marveling at the giant mushrooms all around.

And then, around the base of one of the giant mushrooms, something moved. A small branch twitched, then stilled.

Someone was there.

Someone was watching us.

And by the time I decided to turn and run, it was already too late.

ABOUT THE AUTHOR

Johnathan Rand has authored more than 90 books since the year 2000, with well over 5 million copies in print. His series include the incredibly popular **AMERICAN CHILLERS, MICHIGAN CHILLERS, FREDDIE FERNORTNER, FEARLESS FIRST GRADER,** and **THE ADVENTURE CLUB.** He's also co-authored a novel for teens (with Christopher Knight) entitled PANDEMIA. When not traveling, Rand lives in northern Michigan with his wife and three dogs. He is also the only author in the world to have a store that sells only his works: **CHILLERMANIA** is located in Indian River, Michigan and is open year round. Johnathan Rand is not always at the store, but he has been known to drop by frequently. Find out more at:

www.americanchillers.com

OFFICIAL TRADING CARDS ARE HERE!

Collect cards for every book! Collectible cards are available for all *American Chillers*, *Michigan Chillers*, and *Freddie Fernortner, Fearless First Grader* series of books, including very rare and valuable special-issue limited edition World Premiere Platinum Cards! Find out how to get yours at **www.americanchillers.com**.

Johnathan Rand travels internationally
for school visits and book signings! For
booking information, call:

1 (231) 238-0338!

www.americanchillers.com

All AudioCraft books are proudly printed, bound, and manufactured in the United States of America, utilizing American resources, labor, and materials.

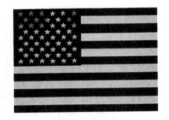

USA